"Since your mind is made up about me, there's no point in prolonging this discussion."

"Why don't you try and change it?" he murmured, his mouth achingly close to her ear.

Before she could catch her breath, his mouth closed over hers and he pulled her into his arms, as if he were starving for her.

"You taste of cocoa," he whispered all too soon. "In fact, you taste of so many delectable things, guaranteed to drive a man to distraction. It's no wonder they're over here day and night.... But you seem to have all the men you can handle right now—" Max's voice had an edge to it "—and I refuse to be part of a collection no matter how greatly I'm tempted."

He grasped her chin and lifted it so that she'd have to look at him. "And believe me, lady. I'm tempted."

Dear Reader,

Welcome to the next book in our exciting showcase series
for 1997! Once again, we're delighted to bring you a
specially chosen story we know you're going to enjoy,
again and again...

Authors you'll treasure, books you'll want to keep!

This month's recommended reading is *No Wife Required!* by
award-winning and much-loved author Rebecca Winters.
Our SIMPLY THE BEST title for November is
Daniel and Daughter by Lucy Gordon. (#3480)

Happy reading!

The Editors

No Wife Required!
Rebecca Winters

Harlequin Books

TORONTO • NEW YORK • LONDON
AMSTERDAM • PARIS • SYDNEY • HAMBURG
STOCKHOLM • ATHENS • TOKYO • MILAN
MADRID • WARSAW • BUDAPEST • AUCKLAND

ISBN 0-373-03477-6

NO WIFE REQUIRED!

First North American Publication 1997.

CHAPTER ONE

"HI, ALL of you listeners out there. Thanks for tuning in to a little Heart Talk with yours truly, Max Jarvis.

"Once again it's time to settle back and get comfortable. Put your feet up, eat a little snack, and concentrate on your deepest feelings about love, romance, and the intriguing, mysterious relationship between men and women.

"You know...in this morning's newspaper, there was an article that gave me a lot of food for thought. I've pondered it all day. According to a recent poll, seventy-six percent of the married women in Utah hold either part-time or full-time jobs in the workforce. The article went on to say that this figure was fairly typical of the percentage of married women working outside the home nationwide.

"I don't know about you guys, but I feel kind of sad about that figure. The world can be a cold, cruel place for a soft, desirable, lovely woman. What do you suppose ever happened to the wife who stayed home to keep the love nest clean, cook delicious, wholesome meals, watch over the children while the husband was forced to leave the comfort of her arms to earn the living? What ever happened to the wife who used to greet her bruised and battered other half with a rejuvenating kiss and a hug at the end of a hard day?"

"*That does it!*" Lacey West muttered furiously beneath her breath, standing on her brakes after roaring into the parking stall of her sister and brother-in-law's condo. While Valerie and Brad were away on business in the Far East, Lacey had agreed to house-sit their place.

As soon as she flicked off Radio Talk, she dashed into the condo, determined to phone the radio station and give Max Jarvis a piece of her mind. In his way, he was quite brilliant, but he'd only come from the West Coast two months ago and wasn't a native Utahn. He didn't understand the real story behind most local issues, which was almost as irritating as his outdated opinions about love expressed on his Heart Talk segment.

She hated to admit that he did have one redeeming quality however; it was a sexy voice. She was almost tempted to drop by the station to get a close look to see if the rest of him lived up to 'The Voice' as she'd secretly named him.

Lacey had a theory about voices. They were more important than faces. She could love or hate on the strength of a voice. And Max Jarvis's voice definitely belonged on her special list along with Pavarotti and Timothy Dalton. Hundreds of new radio listeners attributed to his program had been lured by his voice. They just weren't aware of its seductive quality.

Still, his outsider status rendered him invalid in Lacey's eyes. He hadn't a clue about the history behind the city's school boundary disputes, the flooding cycle of the Great Salt Lake, or the attorney general quitting his post, midterm, to take a higher paying job in the workforce, irritating the voters who elected him.

As for his antiquated theories on marriage...

With the light of battle kindling her forest-green eyes, she let herself in the back door of the condo. George, the lovable, trained capuchin monkey she was tending for her psychologist friend, Lorraine, must have heard her put the key in the lock because he wrapped his arms around her legs when she walked in.

Lacey experienced a stab of positively maternal feeling as she patted his head. "I've missed you, too. Come on. Let's eat. I'm starving."

While she made a tossed salad and broiled a couple of lamb chops, she turned on the radio in the kitchen, then called the station on her cordless phone.

She must have tried a dozen times, but the male callers siding with Max Jarvis had jammed the lines. When she finally connected and was told to hold, there were only three minutes left before he went off the air for the night. She doubted she'd get on.

With George settled in the far corner of the kitchen to eat his greens and sunflower seeds, she put her food on the kitchen table and sat down to her own meal, the receiver still wedged between her ear and chin.

Finally she heard a click. "Hi, Lorraine. This is Max Jarvis."

Lacey took a fortifying breath. Lorraine was the fake name she'd given his producer. For privacy's sake, she never used her own name and picked a different one whenever she called in on a talk show.

"Yes, Mr. Jarvis, I know who you are." The sarcasm oozed out of her.

"I don't recognize your voice, Lorraine. You must be a first-time caller."

His astute observation not only annoyed her, it caught her off guard. "How would you know that?"

"Because yours has a slightly husky quality I find rather unforgettable. I'm right about this being a first for you, aren't I?"

Her jaw hardened. "As a matter of fact you are, where *your* show is concerned. I've called in dozens of times on other shows over the years."

"You've made my day, Lorraine. The owner of the station loves it when I get a first-time caller. Unfortunately we're almost out of time."

"I'll make this quick," she asserted forcefully. "If you want to know what happened to the lovely wife working her nails to the bone at home while she waited for her beloved to return home after a hard day's work…check with his little girlfriend in town.

"The one who didn't have a clue he was married and hoped to become his wife, only to discover too late that the money he'd been spending wining and dining her was the money from his paycheck to support the family, thus forcing his wife to get out and earn a living she could count on!"

"Were you the wife or the girlfriend?" Max Jarvis insinuated in his deep, vibrant voice before she could catch her breath.

His question shot home like an arrow to the heart. Afraid to reveal any more, Lacey hung up the phone, still angry that Perry hadn't told her he was a married

man with children until *after* she'd fallen in love with
him. Never again!

"Ladies and gentlemen, we've just lost Lorraine.
No doubt her personal story has struck a resounding
chord in the breast of those legions of people who've
lost trust in a loved one. A sign of the times? An
explanation for the numbers of married women enter-
ing the workforce outside the home?

"We all commiserate with your loss, Lorraine. If
you can ever bring yourself to talk about this again,
call in and we'll discuss it further. Until tomorrow at
3:00 p.m., this is Max Jarvis with Radio Talk. Have
a good night."

Hot-faced, Lacey got up from the table and turned
off the radio. By now George had gone into the living
room and was watching television.

Still fuming because everything Max Jarvis said
tended to upset her, she cleaned up the kitchen, then
gripped a bulging briefcase to get to work on the accounts for a client who'd opened an extension of his
law firm in Idaho.

By ten o'clock she called it quits but didn't have
the heart to wake George and walk him to his basket
in the kitchen. So she left him lying in front of the
TV and went into the bathroom for a soak in the tub.

Maybe the running water wakened him because a
few minutes later he suddenly ambled into the bathroom and climbed up on the hamper.

"George? I thought you were out for the count. Did
you miss me?"

George cocked his head to the side engagingly.

"Did I tell you we're leaving on our trip to Idaho

Falls day after tomorrow? Just you and me and the wide open spaces. We'll sleep along the way and do whatever we feel like. Of course, you have to remember I have work to do. We can't fool around all the time.''

She studied him while he displayed a splendid set of yellow teeth. Lorraine had been training him to be an aide to an other-abled person. George had the capacity to do a variety of tedious tasks a human would never tolerate.

"So you want to play now, do you?" She chuckled as he jumped down and came over to the side of the tub, tentatively stirring his hand in the water. "Well, I'm afraid you're going to have to wait. And don't look at me like that with those sorrowful brown eyes. I want to relax for a while first. Then it will be your turn.''

George scurried out of the bathroom and came back with his red ball. He threw it in the water.

"That was naughty," she said with mock severity. "Now you can't have it until tomorrow morning. Sulk all you want, but it won't do you any good." She laughed as he covered his eyes with his hands in exaggerated fashion. He was such an endearing little ham. Obedient, too. He didn't make another attempt to get the ball.

"You know—you're not as hairy as I'd imagined. I wonder what it is about you that Lorraine can't tolerate? How sad if she really is allergic to you. Thank goodness you and I took to each other without any problem.

"I've loved having you around, even if you're too

curious for your own good. In ways I would like to keep you, but even if that were possible, someone else needs you desperately, and you're far too expensive." The responsibility of caring for a fifty-thousand-dollar monkey had been weighing on her from the outset.

Lacey patted his silky head as she got out of the tub and hitched a towel around her. "You miss Lorraine, don't you? But you like living with me a little bit, right?" He looked at the water wistfully, then back at her.

"I know what you want. All right. Go ahead."

George leaped into the tub, rolling his ball over and over again, jumping up and down, splashing water.

"Careful, George. You're getting me wet again. Let's keep everything to the confines of the tub. You're too excited. Now calm down. You act like this is the first time. You know the rules."

Lacey couldn't keep a straight face. Laughter spilled out of her, which only incited him to more antics. He beat on his chest.

"You're too much, do you know that? Come on. Play time is over. You've worn me out. Let's go to bed and sleep till noon. Then we have to clean because Brad's boss from Denver will be flying in to Salt Lake some time tomorrow afternoon on his way to Tokyo. You'll have to stay in the storeroom out of sight. I'll bring you a pillow and your blanket. After he's in bed, I'll come out to see you."

As she leaned over to let the water out of the tub, she could've sworn she heard the clank of metal followed by a low groan. It had to have come from the bathroom next door. George looked at the wall, then at her. He'd heard the noise, too.

"Uh-oh," she whispered. "I think my neighbor is trying to tell us something. We'd better not play in the middle of the night anymore or we might be evicted."

Lacey fell into bed exhausted, but Saturday turned out to be even more tiring. George made house cleaning an unforgettable experience. He followed her around and found the vacuum an unending source of delight.

Lorraine had assured her he was capable of vacuuming, it was part of his training. Though he might not be as thorough as a human, he knew to cover the open areas of the floor.

Lacey decided to let him do the carpet in the master bedroom while she finished the dusting and polishing in the living room. With the plants watered, all she had to do was make up the guest bedroom with clean sheets and scour the bathroom.

Not wanting to miss any of the noon news, she carried her radio to the bathroom and plugged it in while she attacked the tub. As soon as George heard the radio, he turned off the vacuum and scuttled into the bathroom to admire himself in the mirror, which covered one whole wall.

It was a good thing she hadn't cleaned the glass yet. Lacey grinned as she watched him kiss the mirror with his mobile lips. She figured he was a normal monkey and missed the companionship of a mate.

It was anyone's guess if his face made him attractive to the female of the species, but she thought him a terrific specimen. Apparently he did, too. He leaned on the knuckles of his hands and scrutinized himself from head to toe.

Lacey got up from her knees and turned off the radio. In her opinion, the Saturday real estate news show had to be the most boring segment of Radio Talk. At least if Max Jarvis had been hosting it, she could have enjoyed his voice.

She eyed George affectionately. "Mirror, mirror on the wall. Who's the handsomest of all?" George bared his teeth in a huge grin now that he had her full attention.

"You know you're gorgeous, don't you? But there's no need to overdo it. I'm already in love with you, you big ape. Now run along while I finish cleaning. With you in here, I can't get my work done. You're far and away the most entertaining and loving rascal I've ever known."

He loped out of the bathroom. A few minutes later she could hear "Mr. Ed," the talking horse, on cable TV. With that much respite she was able to finish the work before getting ready to go pick up Brad's boss at the airport.

The more she thought about it, the more she was determined to keep George a secret from him. If Brad ever found out, he'd have a fit. He'd chosen this condo because of the 'no pets' rule. His fastidious nature couldn't tolerate animal hair. And Valerie would start giving Lacey more pep talks about finding another man to love *instead of a monkey*.

Lacey wasn't against the idea exactly. It was just that she'd never met a man she wanted to spend the rest of her life with. She worked with lots of men in her job as a CPA. That's how she'd met Perry, the liar. Since there was no way she'd get herself into that kind of situation again, she hadn't been looking for anyone new.

Valerie despaired of Lacey's paranoia where dishonest men were concerned, but then Valerie was happily married and didn't realize that there weren't a lot of desirable, available, unattached males in the world who told the whole truth.

While Lacey fixed lunch, she heard a car start up in the other carport. Good. Her neighbor had finally gone out. Valerie had mentioned that a man had recently moved in next door, but Lacey had never seen him. He kept strange hours, but at least he was gone and hadn't complained about the noise last night. "Come on, George. Let's make a dash for it."

She left her half-made tuna sandwich on the counter and grasped the monkey's hand. With her other hand she grabbed everything else she'd need and headed for the carport, which backed onto an access road bordering the complex. A high fence ran alongside the road, affording privacy.

So far, no one knew she was keeping George on the premises. She intended to keep his presence a secret until Lorraine came for him.

The storage shed ran along half of the carport wall. She undid the heavy padlock and ushered George inside, pulling the cord that turned on the light. "See what I have for you." She handed him his pillow and blanket and watched as he made a little bed for himself at one end of the pad.

With that accomplished, he examined the contents of the sack she'd put by the door. Out came his red ball, a hoop the size of a dinner plate, and a handmade seesaw which moved up and down slowly when he placed a marble in the holder.

While he busied himself with his toys, she ran back to the condo and brought out a small, portable TV, which she set up on one of the boxes, hooking up a long extension cord that ran under the door to an outlet in the carport. The television would keep him company if he got lonesome. In his dishes she put water, lettuce, apples, and sunflower seeds. Enough to hold him through the day and night.

"Be a good boy. I'll come in and say good-night before I go to bed. Remember. No hooting or screaming."

She made the sign Lorraine had taught her. George understood her hand gestures and ambled over to hug her legs. "Lacey loves you, too, George. This is only for tonight. An emergency. And because you're being so good, I have a present for you. Reach in here."

She patted the hip pocket of her jeans. George carefully felt for his surprise. He made low hooting sounds when he discovered a strip of beef jerky. He loved to suck on it like a lollipop, and rolled his eyes in ecstasy.

With his attention focused on food, Lacey slipped out of the storeroom and padlocked the door. She felt as guilty as if she'd abandoned a child, but she had to pick up Brad's boss.

To make doubly sure of keeping George's presence a secret, she would park out front for the night. Brad's boss wouldn't have a clue. As it turned out, he was a quiet, self-effacing person in his sixties who just happened to be the vice president of the electronics firm Brad worked for.

He'd put up Brad many times when her brother-in-law had meetings in Denver. Under the circumstances, taking him to the Utah Jazz basketball game turned out to be a stroke of genius. John Stockton and Karl Malone, two Olympic basketball players from Utah, had been at their best. If taking Brad's boss to the game helped her brother-in-law up the corporate ladder, so much the better.

She had been wise to keep George out of sight, but the poor thing must've thought she had gone for good. As soon as her guest left the next morning in a taxi, Lacey jumped out of bed, threw on a robe over her nightgown and hurried out to the carport. No telling how long the monkey had been awake. She could hear the TV. It sounded like the Salt Lake Tabernacle Choir.

George grabbed her around the legs when she opened the door. "I've missed you, too." She patted his head before poking hers outside the door to see if the coast was clear.

Her neighbor's blue Saab was now parked in the other carport, but she'd seen no sign of life. "Come on, George. We need to make another run for it."

He required no urging and reached the kitchen before she did. Once his breakfast was prepared, she returned to the storeroom and cleaned up. With the TV in one arm, his sack of toys and dishes in the other, she somehow managed to lock the door and make it back inside the condo without being observed.

While George watched TV, she left for church, slipping out the front door carrying a sack of smiley faces for the children in her Sunday school class. They loved wearing them on their foreheads if they'd been good.

No sooner had she returned from church than the man from the car rental appeared at her front door. Because of the situation with George, her client had rented her a motor home so that she and George could use it in place of a hotel room while she was in Idaho.

She parked her own car in the carport, then wrapped George in a blanket and carried him out to the motor home as if he were her baby. She couldn't take chances on anyone from the condo seeing him. Once their bags were on board, she drove the man back to the rental agency, then she and George were on their own.

Lacey loved driving the motor home. Because she was on the shorter side, she'd always wondered what it would feel like to sit in a semitrailer and figured it would be like this. King of the road.

One thing about her client. He never did anything by half measures. He had leased her the best Winnebago on the lot. It had everything. Sleeping for six, a shower, galley, TV, VCR, radio, and a dinner table with blue and white curtains at the windows.

Though strapped in the car seat, George was in heaven. She was pretty happy herself and flicked on the radio, excited at the prospect of listening to Max

Jarvis display his ignorance in matters of love once more.

A guest was speaking. "...So it makes sense that living together is the only way to find out certain things which would never be learned in a dating relationship."

"You mean like discovering that your girlfriend had a snoring problem," Max Jarvis interjected.

"Snoring, talking in your sleep, walking in your sleep. The list is endless, and so are the surprises which often cause newlyweds to end up in divorce."

"You make a good practical point, Dr. Ryder. You constantly hear married people say that the honeymoon was ruined by something unexpected, which in turn set a negative tone for the marriage. It looks like the board is lit up with callers wanting to talk to you.

"Ladies and gentlemen, this is Max Jarvis and we have Dr. Victor Ryder in studio for the next half hour, anxious to discuss his new book entitled, *Living Together. A solution for the technological age.* Hello, Phil."

Lacey brought the motor home to a shrieking halt. George hooted.

"Sorry, but that man makes me so angry I missed the turnoff for Malad. We'll have to backtrack to Garland."

For 'The Voice' to agree with some one-book-wonder marriage therapist on the subject of living together made Lacey's blood boil. Especially someone like Victor Ryder. The name was all too familiar to Lacey and if he was a legitimate therapist she was Madonna! How could Max Jarvis be such a fool?

Why didn't he go back to California where he belonged?

She had half a mind to call him and tell him just that. When she spied a free telephone booth outside a convenience store in Garland, she maneuvered the motor home into the parking lot and turned off the ignition.

"I've got to make a phone call, George. You can watch me. I won't be long. We'll reach Idaho Falls by seven and then some. Since the reservations are all made, we won't have to worry where to park when we get there."

As she left the motor home, a couple of kids were coming out of the store. When they saw George perched near the front dashboard they asked Lacey if she minded if they watched him while she made her call.

She knew how they felt. Apes had always been her favorite animal at the zoo. Maybe that was why she had been so willing to help out Lorraine. Lacey told the boys to enjoy themselves and returned to the business of getting a free long-distance line. After ten tries, she connected.

"This is Radio Talk. Do you have a question for Dr. Ryder?"

"Actually, I'd like to speak to Mr. Jarvis."

"What's your name?"

"Gloria."

"Hold on, Gloria. You'll be up next."

"I'm holding."

Lacey waited another minute, then Max Jarvis's

voice was speaking. "Hello, Gloria. I hear you want to speak to me."

"That's right."

"Where are you calling from?"

"Garland."

"As in?"

"Utah! And if you knew anything about this state, you wouldn't have had to ask that question."

He chuckled. "I may not know a great deal about Utah, but I do know voices, and you're not Gloria. You're Lorraine! I've been hoping you'd call back, but it's been a while and I'd almost lost hope. Go ahead and take all the time you need to vent your feelings about your unsatisfactory personal life."

Lacey blinked in stunned surprise. He was a lot more intelligent than she'd given him credit for.

"My personal life is my own concern. But I do want to vent my feelings about the kinds of outrageous opinions you express, which not only show that you're from out of state, but that you know nothing about men and women."

"So what you're saying is that if a man isn't from Utah, he doesn't know what he's talking about?" he asked in a mild tone, raising her blood pressure.

"Let's just say we were all just fine until you came along with your unique brand of 'practicality'! What really alarms me is your willingness to let anyone who has written a book be a guest on your show. You allow them to pass off their work as the latest authority for the masses to heedlessly imbibe, then side with them when you know there are two sides to every issue! What about romance? What about love?"

His chuckle got under her skin. "Me thinks the lady protesteth too much. Something tells me you've never lived with a man. Is that right?"

"That's right, because I believe in romantic solutions not practical ones!"

"Be more specific."

"If a woman's lucky, she's only going to give herself to one man forever. If a man's lucky, he's only going to give himself to one woman forever. That's the highest form of love, consecrated in marriage."

"Yet your pseudo-doctor guest is advocating that we should be ruled by our heads not our hearts and *you* are condoning it. You're both out of your minds."

"How would you like to put that remark to the test, Lorraine?"

She frowned. "What do you mean?"

"Have you written a book lately on the relationship between men and women?"

"I wouldn't presume to take on a subject that should be left alone."

"Good. Then you're the perfect person to appear as a guest on my show next week and prove to my face that I'm out of my mind, as you said."

"That won't be hard. I'll look forward to it," she averred before it dawned on her what she'd just said.

"All you callers out there heard her. It ought to be an interesting show. Rob—take the information on Lorraine while we go to our next caller."

Lacey knew Max Jarvis's tactics. He hadn't expected her to take up his challenge. She kind of surprised herself by agreeing to appear as a guest on the show. What an irony that after phoning into Radio Talk all these years, she would be facing the one host who had the capacity to rile her.

If she were being honest with herself, she would admit that she really wanted to find out if the man measured up to his voice.

By now, a crowd had gathered around the motor home to watch George. She had to work her way through to climb on board. He hooted a welcome.

"Good news, George. I'm going to be on Radio Talk next week. I've a few thousand things to say to that infuriating man. It's time for his education to begin."

CHAPTER TWO

"Hɪ! You made it. I'm Rob Clark. Max Jarvis will be with you in a minute. I take it you're Lorraine."

Lacey nodded and shook his hand. For the time being, she was stuck with Lorraine's name. "Pleased to meet you, Rob."

She put her briefcase next to a Naugahyde couch. The radio station was a small bungalow situated on a lonely road in the southwest part of the city not far from the condo. There wasn't anything about the place that resembled what she had pictured in her mind throughout her trip to Idaho and back.

"Can I get you coffee, or a cold drink?" He stood there with his hands in his pockets, looking expectant.

"Nothing for me, thank you."

"Is this your first time as a guest?" He watched with avid interest as she sat down on the couch and crossed her legs.

"That's right." Because he was trying so hard, she gave him the benefit of a full-bodied smile. "Do you have any advice for me?"

Her question caused him to blush, which made him appear even younger than she'd surmised. "Just remember this isn't television. There's no camera trained on you, so you shouldn't be nervous. But even if there was a camera, you would have no worries, believe me."

"I agree," The Voice concurred.

Startled, Lacey looked around and found herself the focus of Max Jarvis's unnerving scrutiny.

She blinked. He reminded her of somebody's brother. How many times in her life had she been told that one of her friends had this gorgeous brother Lacey just had to meet? The perfect male. Six feet two inches, dark blond hair, rugged features, blue eyes, lean, a white smile, intelligent, successful.

She'd heard it all, but for once in her life there he was, standing three feet away. And like all things too good to be true, he was probably married with one or two little offshoots showing just as much promise.

A glance at his tanned hands revealed a huge white opal set in antique gold. Not your typical wedding ring, but she knew from listening to his show that Max Jarvis was a man with discriminating tastes. He'd traveled and lived in many parts of the world.

He'd probably picked up that stone in the Australian outback. His tan certainly didn't come from lying around a swimming pool all day.

She happened to know he had recently been on a trip to Alaska. But whether or not he'd gone with his family was anyone's guess. Of all the radio hosts, he was the only one who didn't discuss his personal life, which was an irony considering he loved to discuss everyone else's.

To Lacey's way of thinking, it was a deliberate ploy to keep him mysterious and intrigue his listeners. The ploy worked. He had the biggest following of anyone on Radio Talk. At this point, not even Lacey was immune.

A phone was ringing somewhere, but no one seemed particularly worried about it.

His laserlike glance took in her conservative navy skirt and blazer with a snowy-white silk blouse that tied in a large bow at the neck. There was something intimate about that male assessment which made her heart give a little thump.

His gaze flicked to her face, studying her classic features, the cut of her cap of glossy black curls.

"I guess I'd better answer it," his producer finally murmured, and disappeared.

"Lorraine?" Her host extended his hand as she rose to her feet. "I'm Max Jarvis. We'll be going on the air after world news. If you'll step into the booth, I'll acquaint you with the setup. As Rob said, you don't need to be uncomfortable. If you come across the way you did when you called in last week, we ought to have a lively half hour."

She bit on the velvety underside of her lip with her small, even white teeth.

"It's a pleasure meeting you, Mr. Jarvis, but I have a problem. I came in early, hoping I could talk to you before the broadcast."

Max's lips twitched. "I hope it's not serious," he called over his shoulder as she followed him down the hall and into the booth with her briefcase in hand.

"I'm afraid it is." She sat down in the chair he indicated and opened her briefcase, pulling out a legal-size folder. "This file contains information on Dr. Ryder I think you should see, but Nester warned me I couldn't talk about it over the air."

"Nester?"

"Nester Morgan, of Morgan and Morgan law firm. I'm a close friend of his as well as being his CPA. He said you're free to look at the information. In fact, I hoped you would have time before we went on the air. It's a printout about Dr. Ryder's credentials.

"Among other things you'll discover that his real name is Horace Farr. He's a doctor of divinity, not psychology. There's a copy of his transcript and it only lists a few psychology classes. You'll also find out that ten years ago he was excommunicated from his church for preaching false doctrine from the pulpit.

"If you read further, you'll see that he changed his name and started his own church before this book came out. One of his followers lived with him until she'd given him all her money, then he left her and moved in with someone else. She came to Nester to try to get her money back."

Max took the file from her well-manicured hands and quickly perused some of the findings. After a moment, he sent her a long, penetrating glance.

"I'm amazed you would allow anyone to see this," he muttered in a serious tone. "You must be on amazing terms with...Nester," he mocked dryly. "In fact, you could be arrested if this information were leaked to the public. Why risk it?" He sounded genuinely surprised.

She bristled. "Because your show is listened to by thousands of people who hang on your every word, and I hate it when you go on about a guest when you don't know the real truth. The fact is, you're from—"

"California," he supplied in a testy tone.

"Yes," she affirmed haughtily because he'd made her so mad.

He sucked in his breath. "I bow to your superior knowledge on this one, Lorraine. It appears I'm going to have to be much more thorough in my background checks from now on." He flashed her a quick smile. This time it made her heart turn over. "What else do you have in that proverbial bag of tricks?"

She chuckled softly. "Nothing which could get me into a legal entanglement."

"But I might have to eat crow."

"Maybe a little. I've lived here all my life."

His eyes blazed a hot blue. "And I haven't."

"Correct. And it shows. Dr. Ryder comes off sounding smooth, but his central Utah accent gives him away."

He held her glance until she felt the heat rise to her face. "An honest woman who speaks her mind..."

Beneath his words were serious undertones. A strange shiver chased across her skin.

"All right, we're on in thirty seconds. Pick a subject and we'll talk about it. We won't discuss your views on Dr. Ryder unless a listener brings it up. Fair enough?"

He moved too fast for her. "More than fair."

"We've got ten seconds. What shall we talk about first?"

She seized on the first thought to enter her head. "Football and romance."

One brow quirked. "Something tells me I might be sorry." While Lacey reacted to his quiet irony, he spoke into the mike. "Welcome to Radio Talk. Tonight we have a guest who is going to give me a little lesson about the differences between men and women.

"Lorraine is in the booth now, and I think what we'll do is conduct a poll. For each issue we touch on, we'll have our listening audience call in their vote. Make it a 'yes' if you agree with Lorraine.

"If you don't go along with her opinion, make it a 'no.' I'll have my producer tally the votes at the end of the program. Is that all right with you, Lorraine?"

"That's fine, Mr. Jarvis. But if I get more yeses than noes, will you give me a free sample of that lotion Lon Freeman pushes on the morning show? I want to see if it's really as miraculous as he says it is."

A nerve twitched in his jaw, letting her know she'd said something to amuse him. Unable to resist, she added, "The other day he interrupted a dialogue with an important spokesman from the United Nations, just to advertise it. He has interrupted a lot of famous guests for the same reason, and I can't figure out why.

"He didn't use to do things like that, and I'm afraid he's losing his listeners, which would be a shame since he's always been a local favorite."

"Rob—" The exciting man seated next to her called to his producer. "Why don't we take a poll on that issue first?"

She decided Max was trying to smother a laugh, which relieved her nervousness a little.

"Let's find out if our listeners agree with her. If they do, we'll pass the information along to Lon. To think I believed myself to be the only one in the doghouse with Lorraine.

"She wants to talk about football and romance. I have a feeling we're in for a provocative half hour. Lorraine—" His eyes impaled her. "The audience is as curious as I am to know why you've chosen those two particular topics as a lead-in for tonight's show."

Lacey had to give Max Jarvis full marks for diplomacy. She'd been waiting for him to make a cutting remark about the fact that she hadn't published a book or distinguished herself in any way to merit being a guest on his show.

But he didn't use those kinds of tactics. As far as she could see, he was open, fair, honest, decent, and he definitely lived up to her image of The Voice.

Clearing her throat, she said, "Last week you sided with dozens of men callers who complained about the large number of women who waste their time going to romantic movies and reading romance novels. You said, and I quote, 'The story lines are boring and repetitious because all the two people ever do is fall in love, get married, and live happily ever after.'"

He grinned. "I did say that."

She schooled her features not to let his charisma disturb her train of thought. "The same point could be made that men waste their time watching soccer or football. The plays are repetitious and boring, and everyone knows either side A or side B is going to win. At least in a romance, everyone goes home happy after the game is over."

His eyes were dancing. "That's true. And my producer is signaling me that all the lines are lit up, anxious to jump in. You're on the line, Anna."

It was difficult, if not impossible, to remain irritated

with him. Later he conceded defeat with such good-natured humor, when he asked her to stay the last hour of the Heart Talk segment, Lacey agreed.

Unfortunately she didn't realize until too late that she'd been lured into a trap. The second he opened up the last hour, he went for the jugular.

"I know our loyal listening audience has been hoping to hear more about your painful story, Lorraine. For those of you who weren't tuned in last week, I opened up my show with a statistic about the large percentage of women making up today's workforce outside the home.

"When I asked why more women weren't at home while their husbands faced the cruel working world, Lorraine gave us a very sobering response, then hung up before we could explore her story in-depth."

He stared her down. "With a week to think about it, are you now prepared to tell us if you were the betrayed wife or girlfriend of the man who hurt you? There are thousands of sympathetic listeners out there who want to know."

Lacey's gaze darted to the opal ring on his finger. "I might be persuaded to discuss my story if *you* were willing to let your listeners in on your marital status *first*," she challenged. "You never talk about a wife and family. Does that mean you're not married?"

The brilliant blue of his eyes intensified. "I make it a policy never to discuss my personal life over the air."

"Don't you think that's rather hypocritical when you've just asked me to reveal something extremely personal?"

The corner of his mouth lifted. "Why do you want to know if I'm married or not, Lorraine?"

She sucked in her breath. "I imagine everyone who listens to your show wants to know."

"I find that a little hard to believe since I have no curiosity about the marital status of my callers." His voice mocked. "That's the beauty of Radio Talk. We block out the unimportant and tune in to real issues affecting lives."

"*Your* marital status is a real issue as far as I'm concerned since it might explain your viewpoint on dozens of subjects in which you and I have a tendency to disagree."

"Name one."

"Living together. If you're not married, then I can see why you sided with last week's guest. If you are married, then I don't imagine your wife is too happy with some of your opinions."

"I wonder if my other callers are as curious as you are. Let's go to the Utah county line. Hi, Nancy. You're on Heart Talk with Max Jarvis."

"How are you doing, Max?"

"I'm terrific, Nancy. Now is the chance to get in on this illuminating discussion."

"Say, you know Lorraine has a point. I figure you're happily married, otherwise you wouldn't have asked that question about what ever happened to the woman who stayed at home while her hubby went off to bring home the bacon."

Lacey watched his face, but his expression gave nothing away.

"Are you married, Nancy?"

"You bet ya. Forty years, to the same man."

"Did you stay at home all that time?"

"Nope. He was a truck driver, but we couldn't make ends meet so I drove a school bus nearly all that time to help pay the bills." She paused. "Lorraine? Are you there?"

"Yes, Nancy." Lacey spoke into the mike. "I'm listening."

"Good, honey. You don't have to say anything if you don't want to. I can tell you're in pain. To be honest with you, I guess I'll never know if my hubby ever played around with another woman or not. But if I had found out, I probably couldn't have changed anything, not with six kids.

"You sound pretty young. If your husband did step out on you, he'll probably do it again and again. If you don't have kids yet, then I say leave him if you haven't already, and find a job that will take care of you. Good luck, honey." The older woman sounded totally sincere.

"Thank you, Nancy," Lacey murmured quietly.

"All right," Max interjected. "Let's go to one of our local lines. Hello, Stan. You're on Heart Talk. Have you got something you want to say to Lorraine?"

"That's right. Lorraine? Your voice is sexy as hell and you're probably in your early twenties. I bet you're a real looker and single. What's your take on that, Max?"

Max flicked her a probing glance that made her heart turn over. "As my producer said earlier, if this were a television show, Lorraine would have no problem in the looks department. That's as much as I can legally reveal.''

"Okay, Lorraine. Then let's face it, there are a lot of married men out there who would like to get to know you, but the huge majority will never act on that desire.

"If you're single, it's a given that a small percentage of married men will lie to get what they want. But don't blame all of us.

"If you're married, then it sounds to me like your husband is a fool for straying so far from home, unless you've got something going on behind the scenes while he's out there earning money to support both of you.''

"Single or married, I would never do that to a man with whom I was having a relationship. I'd break up with him first!'' she countered indignantly.

"Unfortunately, statistics don't lie and there are husbands who go home to their wives, only to find them involved with someone else,'' Max inserted so swiftly, Lacey wondered if his remarks were rooted in personal experience.

"It happened to my brother,'' Stan muttered.

"Thanks for the input, Stan. I'm sorry we don't have more time to talk, but the phone lines are jammed with callers and I have to go to commercial. We'll be right back.''

For the rest of the hour, people continued to call in with all kinds of advice for her, and the time was gone before she knew it. The talk show host for the six-to-nine segment had already come into the booth to get ready.

Lacey removed her earphones and rose to her feet, picking up her briefcase to leave.

"Where do you think you're going in such a big hurry?" Max stood in the corridor outside the booth door, larger than life, blocking her exit. "After winning the poll on every issue hands down, the least you can do is have a drink with me on the way home so I'll feel a little better."

"You don't fool me," she murmured. "You loved every minute of your defeat."

"You're right," he grunted. He folded his arms across his chest. "You saw the note Rob stuck on the window. We had a dozen first-time callers. The owner of the station will probably give me a raise. He wants you to come on the show again. So do I. How about next week? The listening audience loved you. You're one of them."

Her pulse was racing too fast. "Thank you, but I'd like to stay a listener. I appreciate you giving me time on your program however. With your sense of fair play, I can see why you were brought to Salt Lake."

Something flickered in the depths of his eyes. "You have my permission to call in any time and tell me I don't know what I'm talking about. That is—" his sensuous mouth quirked "—if you'll give me equal time. I'm off for the night. Will you go out with me?"

A long time ago Perry had asked her the same question and she'd said yes. A month later she found out about his wife and children. Max Jarvis was tempting. She was tempted. But...

"I make it a policy not to go out with a man who can't reveal his marital status over the air." She glanced at her Mickey Mouse watch. After all these years it still worked perfectly, while two other expensive Swiss watches sat broken in her jewelry box. "I'm also a half hour late for home already."

"Another time then," he declared as if it were a statement of fact, then walked her to the front door. "We didn't explore the football versus romance angle enough. I'd like to hear the rest of that argument sometime soon. I'll call you."

She started to say, "don't bother," when she was interrupted by his producer.

"Lorraine—don't forget your lotion. Lon Freeman heard about what you said. He called in to tell me to give you a free sample. It's really good stuff. Try it on your legs. Not that they need improvement or anything."

Max Jarvis's all-encompassing gaze did a swift inventory of her legs, which suddenly felt as shaky as rubber. This time her face went hot.

"Thank you very much. If it works those purported miracles, I'll call in with my own testimonial, but don't hold your breath."

She turned to Max. "Thank you, Mr. Jarvis. I didn't expect to enjoy this evening so much."

A mysterious gleam entered his eyes. "The surprise was all mine, Lorraine. Good night."

Shaken by their meeting, Lacey hurried out to the car and sped all the way to the supermarket located a few blocks from the condo. Every time she thought of Max Jarvis, which was pretty constantly, a spurt of adrenaline shot through her system.

She'd given him a chance to tell her the truth, but

he hadn't taken it. No man that attractive was still single. He had to be married, or living with a woman, she groaned inwardly. To waste her time fantasizing about him would be absurd. The only way to get over him was to stop listening to the radio during his show.

Later, when she stood in line at the counter, a voice she'd know anywhere murmured, "I'm glad I found out you're a vegetarian. I was going to ask you out for a steak dinner next week."

Shocked, Lacey turned around and discovered Max Jarvis standing behind her, staring at her groceries; lettuce, sunflower seeds, greens, and yogurt. Her heart was being given the greatest workout of its life.

Her fear that he might have a wife at home prompted her to put an end to this right now. "Did you follow me here?"

His features hardened perceptibly. "I hate to disappoint you, but the answer is no. This is where I shop."

That was funny. She always bought her groceries here, but this was the first time she'd ever seen him on the premises.

"Interestingly enough," he drawled, "the thought did occur to me that you had followed *me*. Have you changed your mind about going out for a drink?"

"No!" she defended hotly, then had to force herself to calm down. "I shop here, too. I—I'm sorry if I jumped to conclusions."

Embarrassed and out of sorts, she avoided his narrowed gaze and waited nervously in line to pay for her groceries.

"Hello." The cashier grinned at her. "You're looking mighty fine tonight." The college freshman had been trying to get a date with her for the last year.

"How are you, Roger?"

"Better now that you've shown up," he said as he bagged her groceries. "I've got two fifty-yard-line tickets to the game Saturday afternoon. How about it?"

"Roger—I was playing football with the kids on the block before you were born. Try asking a girl your own age."

"Girls my own age don't interest me."

"How many times have I told you that I make it a habit not to date a boy young enough to be my little brother? Have a good evening."

She paid for her groceries and left, all the while conscious that Max had heard every word of their conversation. At least now he knew she was a regular customer at this store and couldn't accuse her of following him.

"You were pretty rough on Roger, weren't you?" came the distinctive sound of his voice directly behind her. "Boys his age have fragile egos."

Lacey swung around in the middle of the crowded parking lot. "His is about as fragile as concrete. He may look innocent, but he picks up desperate older women on a regular basis."

"That's because he's terrified of girls his own age. Think about that and let him down a little more gently next time. Whoever hurt you did a fairly thorough job of it. You've left a couple of bleeding victims in your wake and the night's not even over yet."

A couple of bleeding victims, she grumbled silently

as she wheeled away from him and found her car. A man who refused to be honest about his marital status wasn't capable of being a victim and definitely didn't deserve the time she spent thinking about him....

CHAPTER THREE

"COME on. It's late and I've a full day's work tomorrow. Let's go."

Lacey bundled George in a quilt like a baby and headed home from the park across the street from the condo. She tossed the sack which had contained his dinner into the garbage can on the way.

After having watched him eat greens, the thought of a steak dinner with Max Jarvis sounded more and more enticing. But he'd probably never call her now.

It had been a couple of hours since she'd walked away from him in the supermarket parking lot. If by some miracle he did try to phone her, she would ask him politely if he were married. No sense wondering about the hotshot from California with the hot blue eyes if he belonged to someone else, if not in spirit and body, on paper. No more Perrys in her life. Not ever!

Once again exhausted, Lacey put George to bed in his basket, then slid beneath the covers of her own bed as soon as they returned to the condo. She didn't know anything else till the phone rang the next day around ten. George had been playing with his hoop at the side of her bed and handed her the receiver.

She patted his head and said hello.

"Hi, Lacey. It's Lorraine."

"Hi! How are you? What does the doctor say?"

"That's why I'm calling. He's given me a new medication he hopes will work. He doesn't think I'm allergic to George after all. But he does think the shampoo I've been using may be the culprit. Can you believe it? It's the same shampoo I use to bathe George." She named the brand.

"That's what I use," Lacey murmured, "but it hasn't made me break out in a rash or hives or anything."

"Well, it's only a theory, but I hope he's right. Listen. I'm going to come over right now and get George, keep him for the weekend. You haven't bathed him yet, have you?"

"No. Sometimes I let him play in the plastic tub you brought over. But I haven't let him use the shampoo. The only soap he has touched is that liquid stuff. What do you think?"

"Good. The doctor wanted to be sure he hadn't been near my shampoo for at least a week."

"You're taking him for the whole weekend?"

"What's the matter? Do I detect a note of relief in your voice?"

"Don't get me wrong, Lorraine. He's wonderful and perfectly behaved, but I'm beginning to understand why new mothers always look so harried and exhausted."

Lorraine chuckled. "It's a huge responsibility. I take it you've decided not to volunteer as a foster parent to another monkey."

"I don't think so. He needs a home with lots of room and a backyard where he can play. Every time I get down to work on someone's accounts, he wants to help. I end up playing with him and accomplish nothing.

"But I wouldn't have missed the experience for the world. Someone other-abled will adore him because he's so loving and good. I had no idea how much he craves companionship."

"He's just like the rest of us. Lacey—you're a friend in a million. I'm confident that I'll have George home with me permanently a week from Tuesday. When's Valerie due back?"

"I'm not sure. Maybe a month. Maybe less."

"I'll help you find a new place when the time comes to move. Has George missed me?"

"I'll say. But I think he's had a pretty good time with me."

"That's what I'm afraid of. You've spoiled him rotten, I just know it. I can't wait to see him. Which reminds me. You know that guy on the radio you can't stand? Max Jarvis?"

"Yes?"

"I think he called my house by mistake a few minutes ago."

Lacey sat up in bed, instantly alert. "He called?"

"Yes. He said, 'Hi, Lorraine. This is Max.' And I said, 'Max who?' and he said, 'Max Jarvis. How many other men do you know named Max?' And I said I didn't know any. That's when he got a little testy and asked me if my phone number was the same number he read out loud, and I said yes.

"So he started over and said he was trying to reach someone named Lorraine but he didn't know her last name. I told him my name was Lorraine Walker. He said I was the wrong Lorraine because my voice wasn't husky enough. Then he hung up. He was really riled. Don't you think that's funny? Max Jarvis of all people?''

Lacey closed her eyes. "That's really funny, Lorraine." How could she have been so stupid? When the producer at the radio station asked for her name and phone number, she gave him Lorraine's. But she'd forgotten to tell Lorraine.

"Lacey? Are you there?"

"Yes. It's a long story. Come on over and I'll explain everything, but for heaven's sake, if Max Jarvis should call again, tell him the Lorraine he is looking for can be reached at my number."

The news that he had tried to get in touch gave Lacey a brand new reason to greet the day. She sailed through her chores and had George ready to go when Lorraine arrived.

After hearing the story, Lorraine agreed that Lacey needed to determine Max's marital status before any more time went by. Perry had done too much damage for her to take any chances.

Much as she enjoyed George, Lacey found it liberating to have the condo to herself. She worked nonstop through the dinner hour on her clients' accounts. When Greg, a close family friend from childhood, knocked on the door, then let himself in with a key, she was still doing figures.

"What do you mean you don't want to see *A Majority of One*?" he barked a few minutes later. "It's your favorite movie of all time."

"I know," Lacey sighed.

"And we don't have to hurry home to George. He's gone for two whole days and nights."

"I know."

"So, what do you want to do? We could still make the last few plays of the Utah-Wyoming game."

"If you don't mind, I'd like to talk. I've met this man, but I don't want anything to do with him if he's married."

Greg rubbed his chin pensively. "Why can't you just ask him the next time he calls?"

She took a deep breath. "Because he doesn't know my real name or my number."

"That could be a problem," he muttered. "Why don't we stop being cryptic. Who is it? Another slick attorney like Perry?"

"Actually, it's Max Jarvis."

"The hotshot from California? The one you can't stand? It happened awfully fast, didn't it? Or maybe being on the air sort of went to your head."

She had to admit it had been pretty exciting to tangle with Max in front of thousands of listeners. In fact she couldn't remember a time when she'd been more stimulated. Except of course when she thought about tangling with him without an audience, which had little to do with words and more to do with—

"Take my advice and find a man with a real job."

She had no comeback to that. In fact she'd been guilty of thinking the same thing the first time she'd heard The Voice.

Out of the window she spotted a lighted 'U' on the mountain. It was too late to drive to the stadium. The Utes had won the football game. "Maybe I'll call in

on the air and put the question to him one more time.
He can't very well evade me without his whole listening audience giving him a hard time.''

"You're really gone on him." Greg didn't sound
in the least happy about it.

"Let's just say I'm interested. He asked me out."

"When did all this happen?"

"After the show."

"I don't like it, Lacey."

"You sound just like Nester when he's trying to
come on like my father."

"You need watching. I told Valerie I'd keep an eye
on you."

"That's funny. I told her I'd make sure you got
back together with Annette. What you two need to do
is start having fun together again."

"Annette and I don't have fun. We fight."

"Then think up something wild and surprise her.
For our first date—that is, if we get that far—I'm
going to ask Max to take a scuba diving class with
me. It's something I've always wanted to do. But
coming from California, he probably already knows
how and is terrific at it."

Greg scowled. "How come you never asked me to
do that?"

"Because that's the sort of thing you should do
with Annette. Why don't you call her while I turn on
the radio?"

She hurried into the kitchen for her Walkman and
came back to the living room wearing her earphones.
Greg had buried his head in the newspaper.

"'...All you Radio Talk listeners. As you know,

once a week, this hour is devoted to the outrage of the week. I'm Max Jarvis filling in tonight for Lon Freeman, who's ill.

"I hope I won't be offending you when I tell you that of all the states in the U.S., including the foreign countries where I've driven, Utah stands alone in its insistence to pass in the right-hand lane. The law states that faster traffic should pass on the left, but you Utahns act as if you've never heard of that law. I wonder if some of you would call in and tell me why this phenomenon only occurs in Utah?

"When I came here from California, it was a little like Alice in *Through the Looking Glass*. Everything was just a little different. Your highway sense is unique. My producer is letting me know the calls are stacking up. Let's go to our local phone line first and talk to Mavis."

"Hi, Max."

"Hi, Mavis. What's your outrage this evening?"

"You won't remember my husband Joe who died two years ago, but he felt exactly the same way you do. He used to drive—"

Lacey removed the earphones and reached for the cordless phone. She knew Radio Talk's number by heart and punched the digits.

"Hi. This is Rob Clark. You want to go on the air with Max Jarvis?"

"Yes."

"What's your name?"

"Lorraine."

"Hey—Lorraine. Hi. It's me."

"I know."

"How do you like the lotion?"

Rob had just given her a legitimate reason to call in. "I thought I'd say something about it over the air."

"Uh-oh. Okay. You'll be on after Mavis."

"Thanks."

"Sure thing."

Suddenly she could hear Max's conversation with Mavis and waited until he switched over to her. The thought of talking to him made her heart leap into her throat.

"He would have liked your show, Max. Keep up the good work. I'll hang up now."

"Thanks for your vote of confidence, Mavis. Perhaps before the night is out we'll have some answers. Let's go to our other local line.

"Well, well. My producer says it's Lorraine, our talk show celebrity from last week. How are you, Lorraine?"

She couldn't tell if he was happy to hear from her or not.

"I'm fine, Mr. Jarvis," she answered nervously, trying to ignore Greg's speaking glance.

"You're on the air. Can you talk a little louder."

She cleared her throat. "Yes. This is open forum, isn't it? We can talk about anything?"

"Absolutely." The adrenaline started to flow. "But first, give us your outrage."

My outrage. How perfect.

"Well—you never talk about your wife and family. Does that mean you're not married?"

There was a slight hesitation before he asked, "That's your outrage?"

"Yes."

"Since this is the second time you've asked me that question over the air, I tell you what. If you'll call Rob on the business line and leave your full name and number, I'll be happy to call you personally and answer your question. Does that sound fair?"

She could hardly catch her breath. "How do I know you'll tell me the truth?"

"How do I know you'll leave your real name and phone number?" Guilt assailed her. "I think it's a little matter called trust. If I recall correctly, you told me that my sense of fair play was the reason I'm still on the radio."

"You're right. I did." Her voice shook.

"Let's make a bargain, Lorraine. I'll satisfy your curiosity, and you tell our listeners whether you were the wife or the girlfriend in your sad story. Everyone wants to know. The station has been besieged with calls."

She bit her lip. "I can't talk about it over the air, but I'll tell you in private."

"Terrific, Lorraine. If you'll hold on a minute, I'll have Rob switch our connection to the business line and he'll get your name and number so I can return your call later. At that point, we'll exchange information. Fair enough?"

"Yes. But before I hang up, I just want you to know that I tried the lotion and I love it."

"That'll make Lon's day. I'll pass the word along. Don't be afraid to call in again, Lorraine." After he switched over, she gave Rob her phone number, then hung up.

Max Jarvis's show hadn't been over sixty seconds before the phone rang. Greg threw the paper down just as she put the phone to her ear and said hello. It could be a coincidence and someone else was calling her, but she had a premonition it was Max.

"Hi, Lorraine."

His voice seduced her on the spot. "Hi, Max."

"What are the chances of learning your real name? I don't think Lorraine Walker would be too happy to find out you've been impersonating her over the air."

She took a deep breath. "She's my best friend, and she didn't mind. For the record, my name is Lacey, Lacey West."

"Lacey…I like it."

"Now will you answer my question?"

"I've never been married, and I'm not interested in men."

Her relief was exquisite. "Why didn't you tell me when I asked you before?"

"Maybe I was waiting to see how interested you really were." Which could have been the real reason or not. "Now it's your turn."

"Like you, I've never been married, and I despise men who pretend to be single."

"The man who scarred your soul isn't worth this much pain. Not all men are liars, Lacey. Sunday night I'm having a little get-together with my friends who'll vouch for me. I'd like you to come. Are you free?"

"That depends on the time."

"How about seven-thirty? I'll pick you up."

Lorraine would be bringing George back. "It would be better if I get there on my own because I have a friend coming over. It might be eight or eight-thirty before I could make it."

"As long as you drop in at some point, come any time you like. I live at Oquirrh Park Condominiums. J-25."

Lacey let out a quiet gasp. The phone almost slipped from her hand. *Valerie's condo was J-24. Max Jarvis lived next door*! The blue Saab was *his*!

"Lacey? Are you still there?"

"Yes." Her voice trembled. "I accidentally dropped the receiver."

"For a minute I thought maybe we'd been disconnected. Do you know that complex?"

Now would be the time to tell him they were next-door neighbors. But an imp of mischief made her want to keep it a secret until the night of the party. That way she could see the look of surprise on his attractive face, and hoped it would be a good one.

Running a hand through her curls she said, "Nobody in Salt Lake could live here and not be aware of the Edsel of architecture. Those pseudo-Spanish condos have to be the ugliest in the city." She warmed to her subject. "Only morons from out of state too lazy to make their own arrangements are conned into living there by unscrupulous Realtors charging inflated prices."

The silence grew ominous. "I dare you to say that when the president of the real estate board comes on the air next week with Lon Freeman."

She grinned. "I'm only teasing you, Max. But admit that you were taken in by a Realtor. So was some-one else I know who purchased it sight unseen.'' Brad had bought the condo while he was still living in Denver, just before he got married to Valerie, not re-alizing what he'd bought. "Like I said—"

"I'm from California," he broke in on a gruff note before she could rub it in any further. "Come to my party and give me a chance to change your low opin-ion of me."

"I don't think that's possible now," she quipped.

"Well, we'll never know unless you show up, will we."

She'd show up all right and could hardly wait for him to ask her where she'd parked her car. Now that she knew who he was, she'd figure out a way to stay out of his sight until Sunday night.

"I'll come, but as I said, I might be a little late."

"I'll be waiting."

Some nuance in his voice filled her body with ex-citement. She didn't know how she was going to last until then. They said good-bye and she clicked off.

Greg was visibly upset. "You're playing with fire, Lacey."

Much as she liked Greg, sometimes he could be irritating, like now. It irked Lacey that Valerie had given Greg a key to the condo in the first place. But she didn't have the heart to ask him not to use it. Because his parents had moved to New York, Valerie let her condo be his home away from home, so to speak.

"Hardly. He's invited me to a party at his place on Sunday night."

"That's the night we planned to watch videos."

Lacey got up and headed for the kitchen. He followed her. She spread some veggie cream cheese on top of a couple of bagels for a snack for them. "Call up Annette and ask her to watch them with you."

"Are you mad at me?"

"Of course not. But I think you're being cruel to Annette. She's in love with you."

Greg took a bagel and bit into it. "But I'm not in love with her."

"Yes, you are. And I think it's time you talked to her to try to straighten things out."

He managed to devour the whole thing before saying, "Last week when I asked her to meet me for lunch so we could talk, she bit my head off. Told me to ask you instead. Then she hung up on me."

Lacey put down the knife. "Greg—I just figured out one of the reasons why she broke off the engagement. She thinks that there's something going on between you and me."

He stopped munching. "No, she doesn't. She's known from the beginning you're like family to me."

"I don't think so. I think she sees it as something more. Have you ever considered I might be a threat to her?"

"If she's that insecure, then she's not the woman for me and I'm glad I found out in time."

His mutinous expression didn't deceive Lacey for a moment. The more she thought about it, the more she realized she'd hit upon the truth. "How would you like it if she spent most of her free time at another man's house when she couldn't be with you? Especially if that man were single and available?"

"That's a bad analogy. You and Valerie are like my sisters."

"But she doesn't see it that way and I don't blame her. You're going to have to stop coming over here."

His face closed up and he stopped eating. "Wait a minute. No way am I going to quit being friends with you to please her."

"Listen to me, Greg. You need to put yourself in her shoes and understand her insecurities. The fact is, we're not related by blood and she's having difficulty figuring out why we're so close.

"She loves you. I know she does. I've seen you two together too much not to recognize the real thing. And you love her. So you've got to straighten things out."

He shook his head. "If she can break off our engagement without explanation, then what hope do we have of a future together? Why didn't she say something about you a long time ago if it bothered her so much?"

"Because she loves you," Lacey said with growing conviction. "She tried to accept me, but she found out she couldn't share you. I can understand that."

"Come off it, Lacey." He sounded upset. "I've never done anything to make her jealous."

"But you have, don't you see? The mere fact that you're always over here while Valerie is away is enough in her eyes. Think about it and you'll know I'm right."

To her surprise he wheeled around and started for the door again. "I'm going for a ride."

"Don't drive too fast!" she cautioned. Greg had a history of speeding tickets, his only real vice as far as she was aware. One day his license was going to get suspended.

"Would I do that?" he flung over his shoulder on his way out the door.

"Greg, why not go over to Annette's right now and discuss it with her? Tell her I'll be happy to talk to her. It could turn everything around."

"No way. I've done all the begging I'm going to do. It's her turn to make the first move."

Lacey had been wrong. He had two vices, and the second was pigheadedness. She stood at the door and watched him pull away from the curb, wincing when she heard the tires of his restored Porsche screech. He was the most upset she'd ever seen him.

Greg was an exceptionally bright guy who'd been a whiz kid in college and now worked as a stockbroker, but emotionally, he was still young and had never had a serious girlfriend until Annette.

She closed the door, pondering how she could help the two of them get back together.

Long after she went to bed, she was still awake, her thoughts on Max Jarvis. His bedroom was on the other side of hers. Only a wall separated them. Even though his opinions over the air drove her crazy, there was an intangible something about him that stimulated her, made her want to probe beneath the surface veneer to the man beneath.

As she vacillated over what outfit to wear to his

party, the phone rang. Because it was almost midnight, she picked up the receiver and said hello, expecting to hear either Valerie or Lorraine on the other end.

"Is this Lacey West?"

"Yes?"

"This is University Hospital. I'm calling from emergency. We have a patient, Greg Peters, who's been in a car accident and was brought in with a simple leg fracture. A cast has been put on and he's ready to be picked up."

Somehow Lacey wasn't surprised by the news, and slid out of bed. "I'll be right there. Thank you for calling." She dressed quickly and drove over to the hospital, but it made her angry that he hadn't called Annette.

For the next few days it looked like Lacey was going to have to put up with Greg's company around the clock while he stayed off his bad leg.

Between extensive car repairs and the fact that he had to miss work, he was as grouchy as a bear after hibernation. He needed Annette. Luckily Lacey's work kept her out of the condo most of the day.

She phoned Greg's ex-fiancée with the news, but got Annette's answering machine. Lacey left a long message and begged Annette to come and visit Greg. Barring that, there wasn't anything else she could do about the situation.

To her chagrin, by the time Sunday evening rolled around, Annette still hadn't called or come by and Lacey began to worry that the problems besetting Greg and Annette went deeper than jealousy.

Lorraine dropped George off, and Lacey suggested that Greg put the monkey to work fetching his glasses and magazines, the kinds of tasks he was trained to do.

Greg balked at the suggestion, but for once Lacey paid little attention. Trembling at the prospect of seeing Max again, Lacey checked herself in the mirror for the tenth time, hoping the simple, basic black sleeveless dress with her gold jewelry was appropriate.

When she was ready, she looked out the front window hoping to see Annette's car. People were arriving for the party next door, but there was no sign of her.

"How come you're wearing your black dress?"

"Because it's the only dressy dress I own."

"You're crazy to be interested in a rolling stone like Max Jarvis."

"Until you get your own love life worked out, don't start on mine," she warned.

"I'll go over with you to keep an eye on things. I need to start getting used to my crutches."

"You weren't invited, Greg. Enjoy the popcorn and videos. George will keep you company."

He made a hooting sound before she hurried through the condo to the front door. If she waited any longer, there'd be no party to go to.

CHAPTER FOUR

A MAN named Jeff greeted Lacey at the door and ushered her into the living room. There were twenty or so people, some husbands and wives, drinking and talking against a background of music which sounded like Vivaldi.

After asking her preference, Jeff handed her a cola and introduced her to Nick and Milo, a couple of other friends of Max's.

She didn't recognize any other faces however. Perhaps some of the people lived in the complex, but she hadn't been very social since she'd agreed to housesit the condo.

"So. You decided to tear yourself away from whatever else you were doing. I'm flattered," a familiar male voice spoke from behind, startling her.

Adrenaline surged through her veins as Lacey whirled around to face Max who was wearing a beautiful tan cashmere sweater and trousers. An enticing smile belied his innuendo. He was looking at her the same way he'd done in the parking lot of the supermarket. As if she'd left more bleeding victims lying around without giving them a thought.

His gaze traveled deliberately over her face and body, bringing a flush to her cheeks before he flicked a glance to the drink in her hand. "Surely we've got something stronger than Coke to entertain my guest," he murmured to Jeff.

"I don't like alcohol," she explained before Jeff could say anything. "Coke is fine."

Max's dark blond brow quirked. "Then have some pâté."

"I couldn't. Gr—I've just eaten dinner. Please don't worry about me."

"I want to worry about you. That's my prerogative," he insisted, and cupped her elbow to guide her to the couch. "You've arrived in time to help us preview a film we've put together on the Haida in Alaska."

She shook her head, confused. "What film? Who is we?"

The corner of his compelling mouth lifted. "My friends and I make documentaries when we're not working at our other jobs. The film you're about to see is part of a series we're doing on Natives of the Americas for the International Educational Institute."

"So that's why you're going to the Amazon! Lon Freeman mentioned something about it on his program the other day."

"That's right. We'll be filming the Arawak in the northern territory."

"What are you doing in radio when you're a photographer?" she asked as the rest of the crowd found seats around the large screen placed in the corner.

"You mean, why am I swimming in waters over my head here in Utah when my real expertise lies in doing something else quite different?" The gleam in his blue eyes did not go unobserved.

"I've already apologized for being so outspoken."

"That's interesting. I must have missed it."

She cleared her throat. "We were talking about your work as a photographer."

"Photography's not my line. I do the research and the narrations. It's up to the other members of the crew to take pictures and do the editing."

Lacey had a dozen questions to ask him, but was forced to save them because he moved away to turn off lights as one of the documentary team members started the video. To her surprise, Max returned and sat down on the arm of the couch so his trouser-clad thigh brushed her shoulder. The contact sent a wave of delight through her body.

For the next half hour she sat spellbound as they viewed the breathtaking film and listened to Max's narration about a group of Native Americans she'd never heard of before. Their particular race had Caucasian coloring and lived on a remote island far to the north.

His vibrant voice had a hypnotic quality and she felt a keen disappointment when the viewing came to an end. Everyone had questions, keeping him and the other members of the crew busy explaining until well after midnight.

Suddenly remembering that Greg needed help to get ready for bed, Lacey rose to her feet, intending to thank Max and say good-night. But he was engaged in conversation with a good-looking redhead who seemed to be on more than friendly terms with him.

Max must have noticed Lacey hovering nearby and broke off what he was saying to introduce them.

"Lacey, this is Michelle Logan, a nurse at University Hospital. Michelle, meet a friend of mine, Lacey West. Lacey is a CPA."

Michelle said something polite to Lacey and she said something polite back, but her concentration wasn't what it should have been because she felt unreasonable jealousy over his association with the other woman.

"I'm afraid I need to be going. Thank you for the party, Max. I think your documentary was outstanding."

He eyed her with suspicion. "I think you're being diplomatic so as not to embarrass me in front of my friends."

"No. I really meant it."

"So a man from California *can* do something right. Is that what you're saying?"

"I'm sure you can do several things right."

"Well, thank you. This is getting better and better. I'll walk you out to your car so you can enumerate them for me."

"What about your guests?"

"They'll survive without me."

When they reached the sidewalk she said, "Actually I didn't come in my car because I live close by."

"Then I'll walk you home. Which way?"

"Not very far."

He gripped her arm as they moved toward her sister's porch.

When it dawned on him what was happening, he slowed down and she felt his hand fall away, leaving her bereft. She thought, of course, that he'd chuckle or at least smile at the amazing coincidence. But he did neither. In fact, his face was no longer animated.

"What's going on?" The remoteness of his voice brought her up short.

"When you gave me your address," she began in a quiet voice, "I found out we were next-door neighbors and decided to surprise you. But you don't look very happy about it."

"Perhaps that's because your husband, Brad, told me your name was Valerie." His brows knit together. "How many other aliases do you go by besides Lorraine, Gloria, and Lacey?"

"You don't understand," she cried, anxious to straighten out the misconceptions. "I'm Lacey, Valerie's twin sister. I've been house-sitting their condo while they're in the Far East."

"Really."

Lacey rarely displayed her temper, but she did have one. Right now it was threatening to erupt. "Yes. Why would I lie?"

"Why does anyone?" he returned smoothly.

She blinked. It looked like only a picture of her with Valerie was going to restore him to the person she thought she knew. "There are photographs inside if you need proof." At this point her chin had lifted defensively.

When he didn't say anything, the negative tension increased. More upset than she'd been in a long time, she opened the door to the condo. To her horror, she heard Greg's voice. "Lacey? Is that you? I've been waiting for you so we could go to bed."

Dear God. In such a suspicious frame of mind, she

could just imagine the construction her neighbor would put on Greg's presence, let alone that remark.

Max's eyes became blue pinpoints of light. "No wonder you were in such a hurry to leave my place."

"No—" she whispered, frantic to set the record straight.

"Who's with you?" Greg demanded in a possessive tone.

Her eyes closed tightly because so much damage had been done already, she didn't know how she was going to get back in Max's good graces.

"Aren't you going to introduce us, Lacey?" Greg had finally made it to the door on his crutches.

So angry she was ready to kill Greg, she muttered, "This is Max Jarvis. Max, meet an old family friend, Greg Peters."

Max stood like a piece of petrified wood. Greg nodded. "Hi, Max. Sometimes I catch your radio show. You're pretty good for an outsider."

"For an incapacitated man, you do pretty well yourself." His narrowed gaze switched to Lacey. "You should have told me about your old family friend. He could have come to the party, as well."

"Sorry I made her late, but you know how it is when you're helpless," Greg interjected. "Don't stay up too long, Lacey."

As he turned around with some difficulty, Lacey shied away from those faintly accusing blue slits. "It seems I didn't get you home any too soon."

"Greg is a spoiled child, and has never made the best patient," she muttered beneath her breath.

"How fortunate that such a large child has someone like you to fill his needs."

Lacey blinked. No matter what Max thought about Greg, she was surprised at his reaction. She doubted it had anything to do with jealousy. He honestly thought she'd lied to him. Why would he jump to so many conclusions unless someone he'd loved in the past hadn't been honest with him? Talk about being scarred forever...

"Tell me, Lacey—assuming that's your real name. If I were to suddenly become incapacitated, would you be as kind to me?"

His question caught her on the raw. "Somehow the idea of you being incapacitated for any reason would never occur to me."

"Maybe I'll return from the Amazon with a poison dart wound and surprise you."

"If you are attacked by hostile natives, it will probably be because you said something out of ignorance and they were forced to take action."

His head reared back and he laughed, but his eyes were still unsmiling when he said, "No matter what kind of life you lead, you ought to be working in radio. You're a natural."

The compliment passed her by completely. "What do you mean, the kind of life I lead?"

"Let's just say your life is a colorful one and leave it at that."

"*Colorful*?" Indignation sent the blood rushing to her cheeks. "That's an interesting choice of words considering you know next to nothing about me."

"I know more than you think I do."

"Really? Perhaps one day you'll let me in on it. How soon are you leaving for the Amazon?"

"Tomorrow morning. We'll be gone six days. Why do you ask? Are you a fan of Lon Freeman?"

Lacey's face closed up. "He's an excellent talk show host. But don't worry, he doesn't have your following. Don't tell me you're fishing for compliments when you know that your program draws more listeners than anyone else on Radio Talk."

"That's always nice to hear, considering I'm from California," he drawled.

"I know. Strange, isn't it?"

Suddenly even that brief spurt of levity vanished as he said, "What I want to know is how you're privy to inside information about the ratings."

Lacey had taken enough for one night. "I have my sources, but I must admit I'm surprised you bothered to ask. Considering you know me so well," she rejoined with a heavy dose of sarcasm.

"Lacey?" Greg called to her again.

Max's glance was derisive. "You'd better go in. Your old family friend is making noises."

She wanted to explain that Greg and his ex-fiancée were in the middle of a huge fight, that he would be going back to his own apartment in the morning. But Max had made her so mad, she said something completely different.

"I had intended inviting you in to show you some old family photographs, but I just remembered that you have your own party to get back to. What's-her-name is probably wondering why you're taking so

long to say good-night to such a—'' Lacey paused.
"Colorful person.''

Too heated to remember her manners and thank
him for the party, she hurried inside the condo and
shut the door. By the time she'd reached her bedroom,
she was in tears.

Greg knocked on the door and tried to get her to
talk to him, but she was too hurt and upset to answer.

"Look, Lacey— I know you're mad at me. But I
was only trying to warn him off because I have a
feeling he could hurt you a lot more than Perry ever
did. This guy has really been around. You know? He's
in his mid-thirties. If he's still single, don't you wonder why?''

*Yes. She'd been wondering about that ever since
he'd told her he wasn't married. Something was
wrong with Max Jarvis, but it was none of Greg's
business.*

"Look, Greg, I need time to sort it all out. I need
peace. Go to bed.''

"Hey— I'm sorry, Lacey.''

"I believe you, but right now I want to be left
alone.''

"Okay. Good night.''

Lacey pounded the pillow. There wasn't one good
thing about this night. Her eyes darted to the phone
at the side of her bed. She had to fight the compulsion
to phone The Voice and really have it out with him.
Who did he think he was, throwing around innuendos
that wounded her deeply?

She tossed and turned for what seemed like hours.
At some point however, she must have fallen asleep.

The next morning she awakened still wearing the black dress, which was a crumpled mess. Numbly, she took a shower and got dressed.

There was no noise coming from Max's side of the wall. He'd probably left for the Amazon already. The pit in her stomach yawned wide as she trudged into the kitchen to fix George and Greg some breakfast.

He still occupied the couch, but had enough sense not to cross her in this mood. George was always attuned to her feelings and made low hooting sounds, following her everywhere.

Once they'd eaten, she drove Greg to his apartment in the center of town, made sure he had everything he needed, then headed to Croft's bookstore to bring home some accounts she was working on for them.

It set the pattern for the rest of the week, but Max was gone out of her life never to return, and she felt like she was in mourning.

She kept looking around her sister's condo, aware of a loneliness she'd never experienced in her life. Not even her parents' death had made her feel this desolate. She was almost twenty-eight years old and had nothing to show for it. No home of her own. No husband, no children.

Lorraine would tell her to look on the positive side. She had her health, a wonderful job, good friends and family. It should be enough.

It had always been enough until Max Jarvis moved to Utah and made her fall in love with his voice. Except she was terrified that somewhere along the way, she'd fallen in love with more than his voice and couldn't do one thing about it because he *hated* her.

After another good cry, while George made com-
miserating hoots, she decided that rattling around the
condo wallowing in self-pity would make her worse.
She'd drive over to Nester's and have a good talk.
Then she'd come back and take George to the park.

Later that weekend, Cameron Morgan drove down
to Salt Lake from Idaho Falls and dropped by the
condo Sunday night to thank Lacey for helping him
with the books. When she heard the doorbell ring, she
put George in the bathroom, then answered the door.

Cameron had brought her a box of chocolate truf-
fles, his favorite candy on earth, and hers. She invited
him in and took off the lid just as the doorbell rang
again.

"Excuse me a moment, Cameron." She bit into a
truffle before getting up from the couch to answer it,
and almost fainted to discover Max Jarvis standing on
the porch. In six days he'd acquired a bronzed sheen
and looked fantastic in Levi's and a cream-colored
crew neck pullover.

She felt intense relief that he'd returned safely,
which was absurd. According to Radio Talk, he'd
been traipsing all over the world for a number of
years, doing a variety of things in remote, dangerous
places.

But she hadn't known him then, and hadn't been
captivated by his intriguing personality and charisma.
The problem was, after last week she never expected
to see him again except in passing. Besides thinking
she was a liar, he'd assumed she and Greg were lovers.

His penetrating gaze traveled beyond her to

Cameron, who was helping himself to another truffle. More damning evidence in Max's eyes, no doubt.

"It seems I've arrived at the wrong time."

"You're welcome to come in," she dared him, feeling reckless with Cameron as her security.

"I have a proposition to discuss with you but I can do it another time when you're not busy."

"I'm leaving," Cameron spoke up, walking toward them.

Lacey could have wept because he was deserting her. He smiled at Max, expecting an introduction.

She might as well get it over with. "Cameron Morgan, this is Max Jarvis."

"Any relation to Nester?" Max shot the question at him. To anyone else, it sounded innocent, but Lacey heard the undertones and knew Max was just getting warmed up.

Cameron smiled. "He's my dad. I've been made a junior partner in his firm, and you're the talk show host. I've listened to you on my drives to Idaho Falls. You're great!"

Lacey didn't know Cameron liked Radio Talk. He immediately went up in her estimation.

"You mean, you don't condemn me for being from California?"

"Are you kidding? The talk show hosts from Utah are *boring*. Keep up the good work. Lacey?" He directed his attention to her. "I've got to run. See you in a month. I'll never be able to thank you for helping me out." He turned to her neighbor. "It was nice meeting you, Mr. Jarvis."

Max made an appropriate comment and followed

Lacey inside the condo as Cameron left to go out to his car. She shut the door and leaned against it, cognizant of tension in the air now that Cameron had gone.

"Obviously the natives didn't get you with their blowguns, so you don't need nursing care. Why are you here?" She knew she was being rude, but it was her only defense.

"Where shall I begin?" There was something so suggestive in the question, it sent a major shock wave through her body.

Why did he affect her this way? She'd fought her feelings all week, and now he was back, reducing her to a trembling, lovesick fool.

He finally took pity on her and said, "My boss wants you to make another appearance on my show along with the infamous Dr. Ryder."

Max could have called her or sent a letter. Instead he'd deliberately come in person to torture her.

"You mean, you're really going to have that idiot back on the show?"

"That was our agreement if you won the poll, wasn't it?"

"Well, yes, but—"

"You didn't think I'd honor it."

"I didn't say that."

"But you implied it. Would it make you nervous to appear on the same show with him?"

"Hardly. He's not my favorite person, as you know. Do you think he'll come?"

"He'll have to," Max said with a knowing half smile, "if only to save face. I'm told we've had a flood of calls while I've been out of town. It appears you're a champion of the people and they want a re-match. Will the twenty-sixth be all right for you?''

Lacey nodded. She was pleased that the owner of the station wanted her for a reappearance. But at what risk if she had to be with Max again?

''Aren't you supposed to be doing your show right now?'' she blurted.

''You noticed,'' he said, as if the thought pleased him. ''I stopped over in California to see my father after we returned from the Amazon.'' This was the first time he'd mentioned his family.

''Southern California, isn't it?''

He nodded. ''Laguna Beach.''

She was surprised he would tell her something so personal when he was such a private person over the air.

''That used to be my favorite spot. Why would you ever leave it to come to Utah of all places?''

''I had my reasons. Do you go there often?''

''Our family used to vacation at Laguna.''

''Where, exactly?'' He acted amused, like everything she said was a big joke.

''The Coast Highway Inn.''

''That's only a block from Dad's.''

''The lucky man. Valerie and I often fantasized about living in one of the homes we could see from the terrace of our room.''

''*Valerie*, again.''

It seemed the appropriate time to take one of the pictures off the wall so he could see the proof for himself. He studied it for a few agonizing minutes.

"It was taken in Laguna. We're entirely different except for our looks."

"You mean, her comments wouldn't make the switchboard at the station light up like a Christmas tree?"

Lacey's mouth curved upward. "That's right. We disagree on every issue. For one thing, she thinks you're wonderful. So does Lorraine."

His eyes darkened in intensity before he put the picture back on the wall. "Tell me about Lorraine."

"She's a close friend of my family who took care of Valerie and me after our parents were killed in a train wreck coming home from California."

A stillness came over him. "I'm sorry about your parents," he said in a low voice. "Your aversion to California is no longer a mystery."

"I—it's not an aversion, and I've gotten over the worst of the pain. Were you born there?"

"No. Hong Kong."

"Was your father in the military?"

"No. He worked as an educator for the state department, helping to create teaching curriculums for Third World countries. In my growing-up years, we lived in dozens of countries and traveled everywhere. After Dad retired, he moved to Laguna."

"I've never been outside the U.S., but Laguna must be one of the most beautiful places on earth."

His face reflected surprise. "I admit it's lovely, but I assure you there are islands and beaches in the South Pacific that far surpass it."

She ran a trembling hand through her hair. "I'll have to take your word for it."

"Don't you have a desire to travel?"

"Of course, but my parents were stay-at-homes without much money, and the last few years I've been too busy trying to make a living to take a trip."

His gaze swept over her. "I noticed. Maybe it's time you took a long rest from whatever it is you do."

She stiffened. "Maybe so, but right now I'd gladly settle for a good night's sleep."

His jaw hardened. "So would I."

"What's the matter? Did you catch a strange virus or something?"

"No." His voice grated. "I think I picked up something a little closer to home."

What was he saying. "A-are you ill?"

"In a manner of speaking, yes."

"Have you seen a doctor?"

"A doctor wouldn't be able to help."

She felt an unwanted twinge of compassion for him. "Is there anything I can do for you?" It dawned on her that his visit mightn't have been purely professional after all.

"Don't you think nursing one man with a broken leg is enough to handle without taking on someone else?"

"Greg is recuperating at his own apartment now," she interjected, glad for the opportunity to clear up any misconceptions.

His eyes narrowed on her face. "What about the other man who lives here part of the time?"

Lacey let out a smothered cry. "There *is* no other man."

Max's cheeks had gone a ruddy color. "That well-

shaped nose of yours should be at least a foot longer
by now. Let me refresh your memory. His name is
George, and the two of you enjoy taking midnight
baths together.''

Her eyes grew huge. "Oh, my gosh. You could
hear us through the bathroom wall?" she shrieked.

"Enough for my friends to place bets on whether
you prefer hairy men or not."

"You were purposely listening?" she demanded,
trying to smother her laughter.

"They were helping me fix the plumbing under my
bathroom sink. It was impossible not to hear everything."

At that revelation, Lacey's entire body turned a hot
pink. When she thought of the conversations he and
his friends had overheard, she didn't know whether to
laugh or cry.

"You play a dangerous game. Does Lorraine have
any idea you're fooling around and going on trips
with her boyfriend?"

Lacey was on the verge of hysteria and could
hardly get the words out. "Actually she *does* know."

"Then that's quite a friendship. It puts her on the
same level as you. But just so you know, these walls
are paper thin. Next time one of your lovers comes to
town for a one-night stand, I suggest you leave
George in the storage cupboard without the TV. It was
a dead giveaway."

"You *knew* he was out there?"

His lips twisted sardonically. "I know enough to
realize you've got an interesting business going on the
side. One of these nights I expect the police to raid

your condo. If you're not driving off in a motor home with one man, you're playing father and son against each other."

"They're both happily married!"

His smile taunted her. "That's right. You only despise married men who *pretend* to be single. Why all that righteous indignation over Dr. Ryder when you have someone like Greg Peters probably breaking his leg on purpose to spend a little quality time with you?"

"Your paranoia is showing, Mr. Jarvis," she said through gritted teeth. "For your information, Greg and his fiancée are having problems right now."

A cruel laugh escaped. "I wonder why. When you think about it, it's a miracle you had a minute to fit in my party. But I can assure you, you're wasting your time with me."

At this point her adrenaline was going haywire. "You think I'm after you?"

"If the shoe fits," he replied, baiting her. "It's happened to me before, one of the negative aspects of being a radio personality."

"Whoa... And I thought Lon Freeman had an ego."

"Why pretend to be outraged?" He continued to persecute her as if she'd never spoken. "You found out I lived next door and decided I'd be your next conquest. So you purposely called in on my show and arranged to be a guest.

"Evidently Nester Morgan would do anything for you, even break the law. For that matter, my producer hasn't been the same since he met you.

"But just so you know, whatever it is that causes men to throw themselves at you, you went after the wrong man when you targeted me."

"Really?" she mocked. "Then why did you invite me to your party?"

"Surely it's obvious. I didn't know you were the predatory female who lived next door."

Furious, her hands went to her hips. "Even if I were the *femme fatale* you've made me out to be, which I'm not and could prove hands down if I wanted to, why do you care?"

For an infinitesimal moment, she thought she saw a shadow enter those glacial blue orbs, but maybe she was mistaken.

"I gave you time on my program because I thought you were sincere. It turns out you're as big a hypocrite as Dr. Ryder. It ought to make for an interesting program. See you on the twenty-sixth. I'll let myself out."

CHAPTER FIVE

"NOT so fast," Lacey blurted, interposing herself between him and the front door. She'd never been so angry in her entire life, and the way he was watching her chest heave only added fuel to the flames.

"You've had your say, now it's my turn." With her hands braced against the wood behind her back for support, she called in a clear voice, "George? Open the bathroom door and come in the living room, please."

There were a couple of answering hoots.

Max frowned, suddenly alert. "What was that?"

Clenching her jaw, she said, "That's George, of course. Since you know so much about me and my wicked life, I'm surprised you had to ask."

"He sounds more animal than human."

"Well, George is quite a specimen, but he's also more loving and giving than any man I've ever met. I trust him completely. The problem is, can I trust you?"

He sent her a half-angry, half-puzzled glance. As far as she was concerned, Max Jarvis deserved everything coming to him.

"I must warn you. He loves me and is very sensitive. Some people get nervous around him. Please don't do anything to upset him."

"Why would I do that when I'm leaving?" he muttered coldly.

"You can't go yet. He wants to meet you. For one thing, you're my next-door neighbor. For another, he's been very curious about you. I think it's time you two became acquainted. Come on in, George."

Before Max could put her physically aside, George ambled into the room and made a dash for Lacey. His hooting sounds stopped Max, who pivoted around, his stunned gaze fastening on the monkey who scuttled around him and grabbed Lacey around the legs.

"Mr. Jarvis. This is George."

Max muttered something unintelligible beneath his breath. Lacey started to laugh and couldn't stop. When she finally quieted down, she said, "George is a very special capuchin monkey trained by my friend, Lorraine, to aid other-abled victims. In a few weeks, he'll be going to his very first case.

"She wants him to be totally accepting and trusting of human contact so he'll bond with his patient, so please don't do anything to startle him."

"You think I'm the hysterical type?" he demanded fiercely.

"No. But I just wanted to give you warning."

His brow furrowed once more. "Consider me warned."

"Then put out your hand."

Max did as she said and the short little monkey crossed the distance to grasp his fingers. To Max's credit, he didn't hesitate or back away. After examining him, his brilliant blue eyes fastened on Lacey.

"He's the one you put out in the storeroom with

the TV?'' Lacey nodded. "The one who cavorted with you in the bathtub?''

"Yes.'' She chuckled all over again. "You won't tell the management, will you? Lorraine's coming for him on Tuesday. I've been tending him while she's been recovering from a short-term illness.''

He stared at her for an overly long time, obviously having to make a few readjustments in his thinking. Since she doubted she would ever catch him in such a vulnerable moment again, she took advantage of the situation by encouraging George to run through his repertoire of tricks.

Max watched in fascination. "He's incredible.''

"I think so, too. But please don't tell Brad when he and Valerie get back from Japan. Though he doesn't like animals, Valerie said I could keep him here if I promised Brad never found out.''

"I won't divulge your secret. Perhaps one day Lorraine could be a guest on the show and tell the listening audience about this little guy.''

Lacey's green eyes lit up. "Lorraine would be indebted to you.''

"Does that mean you'd be able to find the time to come with her?''

"That depends on whether or not you still think I'm a liar.''

His eyes were half veiled. "Let's just say that you've given me cause for reflection.''

She had the feeling it was a huge concession for him to make. "I—I'd do anything to help Lorraine's project. She's in the process of starting a rehabilitation center here in Salt Lake.

"When these monkeys are born, they need foster homes to learn how to live with humans before they can be trained to help quadriplegics. There might be people listening to the show who'd be willing to foster a monkey like George."

He stood there with a lopsided smile, letting George do all his tricks again. "To my recollection, we've never had someone in Lorraine's line of work on the show before. It ought to be a hit with everyone." He raised his head. "Even you..."

Their gazes locked.

"You're an intelligent man, Mr. Jarvis. I only meant that when you're talking about local issues, you lack the understanding someone has developed who's lived in Utah all his life."

He eyed her critically. "My name is Max. Has it ever occurred to you that an unbiased outsider can discuss issues without becoming emotionally involved? That way, I can remain objective and listen to both points of view."

"I understand what you're saying, but Utah isn't like a lot of other places. The only way I can describe it is, an enigma within an enigma."

"On that point, I tend to agree with you."

The inflection in his voice led her to believe he was talking about something, or *someone* else. The blood pounded in her ears.

"Excuse me while I put George down for the night."

While she escorted him to the kitchen, the phone started ringing. She reached for it as Max followed George over to his basket.

It was Greg, wanting to find out if he was still in the doghouse with her. She told him she'd have to call him back and hung up the receiver.

"You shouldn't have cut him off on my account," Max drawled quietly from the doorway linking the kitchen to the living room. "I can let myself out." The tension was back.

It had been so wonderful to feel natural around Max for a few minutes, she wasn't prepared to let him go. "Would you like a cup of cocoa with me before you leave? It might help you to sleep."

"I doubt it," he muttered, "but I won't say no to the offer."

Her heart thudded with excitement as she motioned for him to sit at the kitchen table. "Tell me about your trip."

He stretched his long legs in front of him and folded his arms across his chest. "Which part? The hundred degree heat and humidity, the mosquitos, the native guide party which deserted us halfway through the forest, or the accident that broke Jeff's camera?"

Lacey's eyes widened. "No wonder you're feeling under the weather. Does this mean you didn't get your documentary made after all?"

He let out a deep sigh. "We managed to put it together, but I don't think any of us is too eager to leave on our next project right away."

"Where will that take you?" she asked as she put their cocoa on the table and sat down opposite him.

"I haven't decided yet. The Amazon trip concluded our Native series." He put the cup to his lips and drank.

"At least you're in a position to come and go as you please."

His lancing eyes riveted her to the chair. "Unlike you who has an adoring public and would be sorely missed." He was back to that again.

She drained her cocoa, then got up from the table. Meeting George hadn't helped the situation after all. "Since your mind is made up about me, there's no point in prolonging this discussion."

Her pain had come back, worse than before. She washed out her cup in the sink, then trembled when she felt him come to stand behind her. He rested his hands against the counter on either side of her so she was trapped. Her heart started to run away with her.

"Why don't you try to change it?" he murmured, his mouth achingly close to her ear.

"Because it would be futile." Her voice shook.

"That's not an answer. Turn around, Lacey."

She shook her head.

"Shall I tell you why you can't?" he questioned suggestively.

Lacey couldn't take any more and spun around, her eyes beseeching him to be kind to her. It was a mistake. Before she could catch her breath, his mouth closed over hers and he pulled her forcefully into his arms, as if he were starving for her.

His actions took her so much by surprise, she wasn't able to hide the hunger of her initial response. Her mouth opened to him, giving him access.

He groaned as her hands slid around his neck of their own volition. Slowly, the texture of their kiss began to change, to become more charged, more heated and passionate.

Lacey was aware of his hard body molded to the softness of her own, and realized with a shock that she was approaching the point of no return.

"You taste of cocoa," he whispered all too soon, reluctantly putting her away from him, but he still kept his hands on her shoulders, caressing them. To her shame, a moan of protest escaped her throat and she averted her eyes.

"In fact, you taste of so many delectable things guaranteed to drive a man to distraction, it's no wonder they're over here day and night. I concede that I was wrong about George, but you seem to have all the men you can handle right now." His voice had an edge to it. "And I refuse to be part of a collection, no matter how greatly I'm tempted."

He grasped her chin and lifted it so she'd have to look at him. "And believe me, lady. I'm tempted."

Before her eyes could focus, he was out her back door. For a few minutes she had to cling to the counter so she wouldn't fall down.

She wanted to scream at him that there was no collection! Nothing could be further from the truth. In fact both Valerie and Lorraine despaired of her ever having another date again because of her awful experience with Perry.

Yet how could she explain kissing Max Jarvis as if he were her whole world and everything in it? And more, why did he bother to kiss her if he found her supposedly wild lifestyle so objectionable?

With her thoughts and emotions in turmoil, she

turned on the TV, hoping to get her mind off the sensuous encounter in the kitchen. But nothing could erase the taste of his mouth, or the feel of his arms around her. Never at any time had Perry's amorous advances made her feel on fire.

Yet one devastating kiss from Max caused her to lose control to the point that she didn't want him to stop.

A wave of embarrassment washed over her as she recalled her incredible response. At best it was wanton and would have verified his opinion of her as a loose woman.

Did he honestly believe she had affairs with every man she knew? What could have caused him to think that?

Giving up the TV as a lost cause, she turned everything off and got ready for bed, rehearsing in her mind the number of times Max had seen her with the men he'd mentioned. He had it all wrong.

Plumping her pillows for the dozenth time, she willed herself to forget him and go to sleep. But the awful feeling persisted that he'd be the cause of her insomnia indefinitely.

On impulse she decided to phone Valerie in Tokyo. They always talked to each other if there was a problem, and right now the problem of Max Jarvis loomed large on her horizon.

Forty-five minutes later, Lacey hung up the receiver, mulling over her sister's advice. According to Valerie, Lacey needed to find a way to get him to open up to her and tell her why he persisted in seeing her in the worst light. Otherwise how could she ever hope to explore what might be the most important relationship of her life!

For the next few days she thought of several possible ways to approach him, but none of them seemed right. She went about her work in a total funk, aware that he had taken pains to stay out of her way.

The only high point in her week was Tuesday when Lorraine came for George. His joy at seeing his trainer moved Lacey to tears. Lorraine spent the better part of the evening talking about her plans for a rehab center. Her project needed help getting off the ground and that meant obtaining donations and free advertising from the private sector.

For a kickoff, Lorraine was having an open house at the university. Important public officials would be invited to learn about the simian aide program through materials sent from Florida. They'd also be able to observe George working with a quadriplegic. When Lorraine invited Lacey to come and bring her most important contacts with her, Lacey immediately thought of Max and assured Lorraine of her support.

Finally it grew late, but saying good-bye to George wasn't as easy as Lacey had supposed. She decided that she understood what a mother goes through who has to send her only child away to college.

George had been her constant companion for the past few weeks. Now total quiet reigned. For the next week Lacey hardly knew what to do with her new-found freedom.

Since there was no one to hurry home to, she worked later and later hours away from the condo, and fell into bed every night exhausted. But no matter how hard she immersed herself in accounts, the memory of Max's kiss haunted her.

Finally the day came for her to be on his radio show, but she awakened like someone on the verge of a nervous breakdown. She couldn't eat, couldn't concentrate on work.

On impulse, she'd bought a new outfit for the event earlier in the week. It was a dusky pink suede suit with a silky underblouse of the same hue. Feminine and sophisticated, she wanted to look her best for Max. When she finally walked into the radio station reception area, she was feverish with anticipation.

If everything went as she planned, he'd accept her invitation to supper at her apartment after the show. Hopefully she'd be able to induce him to be honest with her and tell her what was wrong, why he jumped to so many erroneous conclusions about her.

Instead of Max, however, Rob was the one who came out to greet her. She hoped her disappointment didn't show as he gushed over her appearance, then introduced her to Dr. Ryder, the phony doctor of psychology.

"How do you do, Lorraine?" The ex-preacher, on the far side of forty, bestowed one of those revivalist-type smiles on Lacey and held her hand longer than necessary, making her cringe.

"I had no idea a woman who looks like you was slated to be on the show with me."

"Don't be too dazzled by her looks." Max suddenly materialized from the corridor. Not one minute too soon as far as Lacey was concerned. "She makes a pretty formidable adversary, as you're about to find out.''

Evidently Max's gaze had zeroed in on that little piece of hand-holding byplay before he darted her a private glance. It seemed to reiterate his opinion that there was a surfeit of men in her life already, causing her spirits to plunge drastically. Something told her the candlelight supper she'd been planning wasn't going to take place tonight, if ever.

Seconds before he'd appeared, Lacey had debated whether or not to pull her hand away and make a scene. But she'd thought the better of it because they were going on the air in a few minutes. Surely Max could see that the other man repulsed her. For some strange reason, he acted as if he wanted to find any excuse not to get close to her.

His less than cordial welcome sent a cold chill through her body. Where before he'd mocked, even been teasingly abrasive, now he was merely civil and polite. The other night she'd wanted to attribute his behavior to the fact that he'd just returned from an arduous trip to South America and still hadn't recovered.

But that wasn't the case, and the knowledge hurt her more than anything Perry had ever done to her.

''If you'll both follow me into the broadcast booth, we'll get started.''

When she felt the older man's hand go to the back of her waist as if it were his divine right to touch her, Lacey jerked away from him. She couldn't stand men like that.

Disgusted by his familiarity, she hurried ahead and

almost bumped into Max in her need to make certain her stool was placed as far away from that lecherous fool as possible.

She put on her headphones and kept her attention focused on their host, hoping he'd soften a little and flash her his heart-stopping smile, but no such miracle occurred. On the contrary, her pain intensified when Max's fleeting glance in her direction registered no special recognition.

Stung once more, she didn't try to make small talk. No one in the world, certainly not the idiot sitting with them, would have any idea that she and Max were next-door neighbors, that she'd been a guest at his dinner party, *that they'd kissed each other with a hunger that still made her blush*.

"I don't see a wedding ring on your finger. Tell me what a lovely woman like you does for a living, Lorraine."

Avoiding the older man's leering appraisal, she muttered, "I'm a CPA."

"Say— I'm in the market for a good accountant. After we're off the air, I'll take you out to dinner and we'll talk about it."

"You'd be wasting your time, Dr. Ryder. Ms. West is all booked up, and we're due to go on the air in five seconds."

Lacey didn't know if Max had intervened on her account, or if he'd seen another opportunity to plunge the dagger a little deeper. In any event, she was grateful for the interference and turned on the stool so she wouldn't have to look at *Dr. Hormone*, as she'd renamed him.

"Good evening, Radio Talk listeners. It's another beautiful fall weekend, and you're tuned to the Max Jarvis Saturday guest show.

"The long-awaited program featuring Dr. Ryder and Lorraine, a member of our listening audience whom hundreds of you over the last few weeks have asked that she come on my show again, are here in studio.

"Because of you listeners, we've brought them together as a follow-up to a former program when Dr. Ryder was here talking about his book, *Living Together. A solution for the technological age.*

"Lorraine, here, doesn't believe that living together is the answer for today's soaring divorce rate. Have I stated your views correctly, Lorraine?"

For once he sounded straightforward, without any mocking undertones thrown her way to injure her. It made breathing a little easier. "I couldn't have said it any better, Mr. Jarvis. What Dr. Ryder is advocating parallels a society where everyone wants to take the easy way out. No one wants to give, to sacrifice, to commit.

"His way provides instant gratification and an instant bolt-hole when the going gets tough. Unlike the line from Macbeth, he can say, 'Out damn spot,' and it's out. Finished. Kaput. Of course, no one's worried about the child of this fleeting relationship whose world is instantly shattered by this practical arrangement..."

"Mr. Jarvis— If I may break in," Dr. Ryder interrupted. "I believe our charming guest has missed the point of my book entirely. I, too, advocate marriage, but only after a couple has learned everything possible about each other first, before taking sacred vows.

"In some island societies, a couple spends time in the Big House before the marriage to find out if they are truly compatible. It is an age-old method of discovery."

Lacey shook her dark, curly head. "It's a bunch of bull, probably propagated by a bunch of sex-starved men who will find any excuse under the sun to stay single as long as possible and still enjoy everything a woman has to offer. Give me a break, Dr. Ryder.

"None of those men out for discovery ever had the raising of a child on the brain while they tested the many waters available to them. Do you honestly think that if a man went to the 'Big House' with his favorite female of the moment, and she suddenly had a stroke that paralyzed one side of her body, that he'd even stick out the prescribed two weeks, let alone the rest of his life with his suddenly blemished beloved? I've seen that movie, too, and the answer is no. He'd walk away from her and never look back. So much for your test before marriage bologna."

Lacey had gotten so carried away, she'd almost forgotten where she was. When she looked up, she could see Max's shoulders shaking. In fact he was having difficulty suppressing his laughter while he talked into the mike.

"My producer says the switchboard is lit up like a Christmas tree." More laughter rumbled out of him, warming her heart. "I think it's time to take a few calls. You're on the air, Donna."

"Wow, that's socking it to him, Lorraine. You said

it like it really is. You know what's the trouble with this generation? The world is now the 'Big House.' You know exactly what you're talking about, honey, and don't you let anyone tell you any different. Hang in there, girl. We love ya."

"Thanks for the vote of approval, Donna."

"Let's go to the next caller. Hi, Ron. You're on Radio Talk."

"I think it's time somebody got Lorraine in the 'Big House' before she goes shooting off her mouth about stuff she doesn't know anything about."

Max flicked her an enigmatic glance. "Is that right, Lorraine?"

"I'm glad I don't know anything about it," she asserted proudly. "It's going to be a lot more fun learning everything there is to know with my lawfully wedded husband. I happen to think it's pretty exciting to be the only girl who hasn't been around the block yet."

"If that's true, young woman, then you're a true anachronism of our age," Dr. Ryder spoke up, his eyes assessingly candid.

"Spare me the rhetoric, Dr. Ryder. There are still lots of women like me out there, and men, too. We think in terms of the lifetime experience, not in increments of seconds, hours, or days."

Her gaze focused on Max, who'd turned his head to the side and was staring at her. "There are some of us out there," she continued, hoping she was reaching him, "who actually plan to go the whole nine yards with the spouse we originally marry. That includes imperfections, old age, flat feet, heart attacks and all.''

After a palpable pause he shifted in the chair and murmured, ''We have a Utah county caller on the line. Hello, Mark.''

''Say, Max, you've got yourself quite a show. I happen to agree completely with everything Lorraine has to say. With the governorship up for grabs next election, I think I'll write in Lorraine's name.''

To Lacey's satisfaction, calls like that kept pouring in. Only one more person voted for Dr. Ryder. It was a woman, probably the one he was living with at the moment.

Max didn't look at her again. In fact, those few moments where she'd felt a rapport with him seemed to have gone as if they'd never happened. The second he started winding up his program, she slipped past Dr. Ryder like a shot and hurried out of the building to her car.

After the little speech she'd given to Max over the airwaves, if he still had problems believing she was a good, worthy person, then he wasn't the man for her and the sooner she stopped thinking about him, the better.

Deep in thought over the mysterious reason why he didn't seem to approve of her, she hadn't realized that a blue Saab had been following her home. To her shock, Max pulled into his stall and got out of his car at the same time she did.

''Where's the fire?''

Maybe she'd gotten to him after all. With this suffocating feeling in her chest, she turned to him. "I didn't want to have to talk to Dr. Ryder."

"You ruined his plans running out on him like that."

With those cruel words, her hopes for a little understanding were irrevocably dashed.

"I thought we were through and I needed to get home."

"Though the poll was meant in fun, I have a feeling you could run for governor and probably win."

"I already have a job I like. Thank you for allowing me to express my opinions over the air."

"You handled Dr. Ryder like a pro. I wouldn't be at all surprised if the owner of Radio Talk asks you to do a permanent guest spot."

"I'm much too busy and am afraid I'd have to turn him down."

"Because your friend Greg still requires your nursing services?"

She should have expected a remark like that, but it didn't stop her from bleeding profusely.

Eyeing him one last time she said, "Why ask me when you have all the answers, Mr. Jarvis? That's the reason why you're the most popular host on Radio Talk."

So saying, she started to close the door, but he was too quick for her and inserted himself in the aperture.

With their faces inches apart, she could hardly breathe. His eyes were like hot blue coals. For endless moments they played over her upturned features, burning her alive.

"Maybe you see Greg as an old family friend, but

he sees you as something much more. Do the kind
thing and let him go.''

He kissed her hard on the mouth, then disappeared
into his own condo, leaving her in a state of shock.

Though she knew he was wrong about Greg, he had
just said that he believed her. It was a beginning of
sorts.

She could hardly take it in, and wished she had the
nerve to go over to his condo and ask him to spend
the rest of the evening with her.

The next four days were pure torture while she vacillated about contacting him. Finally, when she
couldn't stand it any longer, desire drove her to the
phone and she called in on his program.

Her heart was beating so fast, she was almost sick
to her stomach with fear, excitement and longing all
rolled into one knot.

CHAPTER SIX

"AMAZING truism of life that no matter who you are, no matter what your circumstances, you were born single. Not until much later did some of you get married. It's entirely possible that even if you did marry, you'll probably die single.

"Though marriage is the accepted institution for a certain percentage of people during a certain period of time, being single is still the universal condition of the human race.

"No doubt to love and be loved for a lifetime would be wonderful. But marriage has never been right or possible all of the time for everyone all of the time. So, if you're single, it only makes sense to live the richest, fullest life you can, because you might not ever share it with anyone else in the married sense.

"It may surprise some of you out there, but not every single person has a secret wish to be married. Now that the phones are ringing off the hook, let's find out what you people have to say about this topic. Go ahead caller. I can't read your name, but you're on the air."

Lacey was third in line to talk. While she listened to the radio and waited for her turn, she couldn't help but wonder if Max had just given her the reason why he had never married. *Because he had no desire to be married*? Was he one of that small percentage of people who had no burning compulsion to be locked into a relationship?

It seemed like every time she thought she'd reached a breakthrough with him, he threw her a curve from which she couldn't recover.

Because of a seven second delay, she could hear the caller's comments before Max switched to her line.

"I understand we have Lorraine waiting. I hope all of you Lorraine fans out there are listening. Rumor has it she's out for my job rather than the governorship. Hello, Lorraine."

He sounded his friendly, charming self, but if she could see his eyes, she would know if her call had caused an emotional reaction inside him.

"Good evening, Mr. Jarvis. Whoever started that rumor is insane." An answering chuckle lifted her spirits. "One of the reasons I called in was to let you know that I agree with your opening monologue." She prayed she sounded as cool and collected as he did.

"Did I hear you correctly, Lorraine? Did you folks in the listening audience hear that? Lorraine actually agreed with something I said. You've just made my day."

"It's pretty hard not to agree considering singlehood is becoming the norm in our country."

"You folks heard it on Radio Talk. Lorraine paid me her first compliment. I think this calls for some kind of celebration."

"As a matter of fact, the second reason I phoned has to do with a celebration of sorts. Something the listeners ought to be aware of. Is it all right to mention it over the air?''

''I've had to bow to your superior knowledge on any number of topics. So I believe I'm safe in allowing you to say what's on your mind without worrying you'll be out of line with the station's policies.''

She took a steadying breath. ''An open house to learn about the simian aide program is going to be held on the University of Utah campus, Building 2-A, this Saturday from two until nine p.m.

''Dr. Walker, head of the program for the rehabilitation of quadriplegics, will demonstrate the skills of a specially trained monkey named George. The public is invited to attend and become better informed about this worthwhile and innovative program.''

''I'm glad Lorraine brought this up,'' Max interjected. ''I've met George and he's a very entertaining fellow. Lorraine, why don't you tell the listening audience some of the things he can do for an other-abled person.''

Lacey could have hugged him for giving her precious time over the air to plug Lorraine's project. No matter that her personal relationship with Max was a disaster, he didn't let that interfere with his professionalism.

''A trained monkey can impact on the quality of a quadriplegic's life. Besides offering companionship, which includes touching and loving, it can bring food to the feeding tray, fetch, carry, find anything. When the other-abled person has to be alone all day, the monkey can help him or her accomplish basic tasks.

Its performance reliability is proven to be close to one hundred percent."

"Are there many quadriplegics interested in having a monkey to help them?"

"Dr. Walker says they've had over six hundred requests at their institute in Florida."

"Are there that many trained monkeys available?"

"No. Not at all. That's why Dr. Walker wants the public to become more informed and help fund a program to procure more."

"Through monetary donations?"

"The program needs money, of course. But it also needs volunteers who'll become foster parents to monkeys before they're trained."

"You've all heard Lorraine's comments, listeners. We'll have to make time on our weekend guest program to discuss this fascinating subject in more detail with Dr. Walker.

"But to prove that Radio Talk always supports a good cause, I'll make the commitment to attend the open house on Saturday night at the university, provided Lorraine shows up with me. A lot of our listeners have been anxious to meet her in person. Now's their opportunity. How about it, Lorraine?"

A strange little thrill traveled through her body. "This is such a worthy cause, I hope to see as many people there as possible. Even you, Mr. Jarvis."

"Folks? You heard her say it. Stay on the line, Lorraine. My producer needs to get a few more specifics from you. We're switching to the Wall Street News."

Lacey waited for Rob to come on the line, unable

to believe that Max had finally made a date with her, one he couldn't back out of.

"Lacey? Are you still there?"

It was Max.

"Y-yes."

"Good. I only have a second. In case I don't see you before, plan to be ready to leave the condo at six on Saturday night. We'll go to the open house in my car. Now I have to run." There was a click and the line went dead.

Lacey's hand gripped the receiver tightly. She had no idea how she was going to last three more days.

Promptly on the dot of six Saturday night, the doorbell rang. Lacey smoothed the sweater in a peridot hue over the hips of a matching wool skirt one more time before answering it.

To her dismay her green eyes, so near in color to the outfit she'd chosen, shimmered like the jewels sparkling on the yoke of her sweater. Her cheeks had so much color, she needed no blusher. Max would be aware of her heightened excitement. Nothing escaped his notice.

Wishing she could calm the pounding of her heart, she took a deep breath before opening the door. When she saw him, a soft gasp escaped her throat.

Tonight Max was impeccably dressed in a midnight-blue suit made more formal by the dazzling white shirt and elegant silk tie he wore in shades of blues and grays.

With his rugged features and build, he looked wonderful in any type of clothing, but tonight the impact of his undeniable male attraction left her weak.

At first she'd been so busy studying him, it didn't register that his eyes had been making their own intimate appraisal. Since opening the door, neither of them had said anything, and she was suddenly conscious of the unnatural quiet.

"Hello," she finally managed in a husky voice. For some reason she couldn't think, let alone talk. She had to hold on to the doorknob for support.

"My sentiments exactly," he muttered beneath his breath, but she heard him. The tension between them was palpable. She was afraid to look in his eyes for fear he'd see the light in her own. "Are you ready?"

"Yes." The word came out on a mere whisper.

He said something she couldn't quite catch and raked a hand through his dark blond hair, disheveling it. "Let's go." He sounded as out of breath as she felt.

The cool night air caressed her hot skin as he slid a firm hand around her upper arm and escorted her to his Saab parked out in front. She'd forgotten about the low bucket seats and blushed when her skirt rode up her thighs as Max helped her inside the car.

His gaze lingered on the expanse of her shapely legs encased in the sheerest hosiery. After witnessing her struggle to pull down her skirt, he shut the door.

While he went around to his side, she drew in a shaky breath and detected the subtle scent of rich leather and the musk after-shave he wore. Her senses had come alive to everything about him. She felt as if she were swimming, drowning in his aura, and didn't know what to do about it.

He levered himself in the driver's seat and shut the door, but didn't start the motor. He turned to her with a sober expression. "Shall we go to the open house, or simply drive off into the sunset?"

Her eyes closed involuntarily. She was beginning to believe that the kiss at her back door had affected him almost as much as it had her. Part of her wanted to tell him to take her wherever he wanted, do whatever he wanted, but of course she couldn't say that.

"I'm afraid you'd disappoint all your talk show fans if we didn't make an appearance, and I don't think Lorraine would ever forgive me." By some miracle, her voice sounded steady.

He continued to stare at her for a long moment before starting the car. "Your loyalty to those people you care about is nothing short of astounding."

His comment could be taken in a number of ways. In a shaken voice she explained. "Lorraine held my life together after Mom and Dad died. There isn't enough I could do to repay her," she said vehemently.

Silence followed.

"I meant it as a compliment, Lacey. Perhaps it would be better if we didn't talk. I know another way to communicate which is infinitely more satisfying, and there's no way of misinterpreting the meaning."

In the next instance Lacey found herself being kissed with the kind of passion she'd been dreaming about. Despite the gear shift, he managed to crush her in his arms. She lost all cognizance of the world around her while Max gave her one soul-destroying kiss after another. The pleasure was so exquisite she moaned in ecstasy, and heard an answering sound deep in his throat.

"We're going to be late," he whispered feverishly against her perfumed throat. "How am I going to let you go? The way I'm feeling right now, there's only one place I want to take you, and that's back inside my condo."

Lacey wanted that, too. They had reached a point where logic and duty meant nothing in the face of this kind of rapture. Thank heaven for the confines of his car, which prevented the total closeness she was craving.

"W-we can be together tonight, after the open house." Her stammer revealed the hectic state of her emotions.

"I'm counting on it," he emoted in a fierce tone before devouring her once more. Then he put her swiftly away from him and started the engine.

After that experience, her body was too highly charged to make polite conversation. Judging by the tautness of his physique, he was similarly afflicted. They traveled to the university in an unnatural silence all the more devastating because Lacey could do nothing about this explosion of feeling until much later in the evening.

To her gratification however, it appeared Max's repeated announcements about the open house had achieved results because there was a crowd of people in the lounge of the building when they arrived ten minutes later.

It didn't surprise Lacey that the minute they walked

through the doors, Max relaxed enough to don the mantle of the famous talk show host everyone admired. His smooth polish and sophistication drew people in swarms. For twenty minutes or so he signed autographs. Several people asked Lacey for hers.

Lorraine waved when she saw them being mobbed, and made her way toward them. She was an attractive single woman in her fifties who had worked for Lacey's father, then went on for her graduate degree in psychology. Lacey admired her tremendously, and made up her mind to emulate Lorraine's most sterling quality of selflessness in her own life.

Lorraine slid an arm around Lacey's waist and hugged her, but her gaze went to the man at her side. "You're Mr. Jarvis! It's *you* I have to thank for the crowds that have flowed through here nonstop since we opened."

She extended a hand to him, beaming. "I'm still trying to think of a good way to repay you. Already the donations have far exceeded the amount I anticipated."

"The thanks go to Lacey," he said sincerely. "If she hadn't told me about you and introduced me to George, I wouldn't have known to advertise your project over the radio."

"Lacey's a treasure." She hugged her again. "Why don't you two come in the other room? George has been performing with Ray, the quadriplegic who's been waiting three years for him to be trained.

"So far, George has behaved beautifully. Even after long hours, he has shown no sign of tiring. It's this demonstration that convinces people a monkey can be taught to aid the other-abled.''

Max plied Lorraine with questions as he cupped Lacey's elbow and they proceeded to accompany her to the other room. Lacey could scarcely concentrate on their conversation while Max held her firmly at his side, almost as if he thought she'd try to run away.

"I understand you have a need for volunteer foster parents. Why don't you and Lacey plan to be guests on my show next Sunday night as a follow-up? We could take calls from people who might be interested.''

Lorraine looked nonplussed. "I won't say no to an offer like that, Mr. Jarvis. You're the answer to a maiden's prayer.''

His white smile set off by his bronzed skin caused Lacey's pulse to race. "We'll see,'' came the cryptic comment.

Lacey didn't have to look at him to understand the full significance of that remark. If Lorraine was aware of the undercurrents, she didn't let it show.

The amphitheater held three hundred spellbound people. To Lacey's delight, almost every seat appeared to be taken. Lorraine led them down the stairs to the front where Ray lay on a raised bed, painting a specially rigged canvas with a brush held between his teeth. When he needed a different color, George would take the brush out of his mouth, put it back on the tray, and find another brush to insert.

Tears moistened Lacey's eyes as she watched the gallant effort Ray made while George waited nearby to help. Already man and monkey had established a harmony which was easily discernible.

In an unguarded moment Max's eyes found Lacey's and they communed in silence. Max, too, could see that something remarkable was happening here.

Lorraine motioned for them to sit down next to her on the front row seats she'd been reserving for them. Suddenly there was a murmur from the audience as George left his post and scurried across the platform toward Lacey.

The next thing she knew, he'd scrambled on her lap and was making low hooting sounds. Her arms hugged him automatically and to her embarrassment, she began to cry. She couldn't help it.

Lorraine got up and explained to the crowd what had happened and why, proving her point that monkeys gave love to the people who loved them.

Everyone started to clap. When the din subsided, Lorraine told George to go back to the platform and help Ray. The monkey did as he was told, but every so often he would turn his head and hoot at Lacey, which produced sympathetic laughter from the interested onlookers.

Max thrust a white handkerchief into her hands, which she gratefully accepted. After wiping her eyes, she put it in her purse and sat back. It was then that she felt a hand cover hers on top of her thigh, sending a languorous warmth through her body. He left his hand there for the remainder of the demonstration.

When it was time for the next group of people to be seated, Max helped her to her feet, still clasping her hand as if he had no intention of letting it go.

Slowly they made their way back to the lounge, besieged on every side by talk show listeners who wanted the chance to meet Max in person.

Lacey could see he was fully occupied, and assumed he wouldn't be able to leave for a while. But in this assumption she was wrong.

"Let's go," he whispered in her ear, sending a frisson of delight across her cheek and neck. He literally dragged her with him and all she could do was wave at Lorraine, who smiled back at her from a distance.

He ushered her to his car in short order and once they were inside, regarded her gravely. "How would you like to drive up Millcreek Canyon? There's a wonderful steak house that stays open until midnight."

Lacey knew the restaurant he was referring to. It had a cozy, intimate atmosphere. "I'd love it. A friend of mine performs there on weekends. He's a terrific country-western singer."

"On second thought, I'm too hungry to wait that long to eat." Without consulting her further, he started up the car and they were off. Maybe it was the dark confines of the interior, but she thought his features seemed to harden. The rapport she'd felt with him all evening had vanished. Before she knew it, they had arrived at an authentic French restaurant near the center of town renowned for its veal.

Lacey's nerves were on edge, robbing her of her normal healthy appetite. She ordered a slice of mushroom quiche, fully expecting Max to eat a five-course dinner. But to her surprise, he asked for a side order of *boeuf bourguignonne* and coffee.

They were served almost immediately, which was a good thing since Max didn't appear capable of making anything more than desultory conversation.

Once the bill was paid, he pinned her with an unfathomable gaze. "What I witnessed tonight at the university has given me an idea I'd like to discuss after we get back to the condo. That is, if you don't have someone waiting for you at home, or coming by later."

"After what happened earlier in your car tonight, you *know* I don't," she declared hotly. "Ever since I mentioned knowing that singer, you've been different. Why, Max? He's not a boyfriend, if that's what you're thinking. If he were, I'd be with him, not you."

She heard his sharp intake of breath. He shoved his chair back and got to his feet. "You deserve an explanation, but this is not the place to conduct the conversation I have in mind. Let's get out of here."

Once again he was ushering her to the car and they drove home in tension-filled silence. Lacey's mouth went dry as she contemplated being alone with him, let alone what he had to say to her.

They reached Oquirrh Park in record time. He pulled into his carport, then came around to help her out of the Saab. On trembling legs she accompanied him inside his condo. He switched on the kitchen light so they could make their way to the living room.

At his housewarming party, there'd been too many people for Lacey to appreciate the decor. Now she could see it was attractively furnished in walnut tones and glass, graphics, deep leather chairs and an entire wall of books.

"What will you have to drink?" he asked as he took off his coat and tie. While she sat down in one of the chairs, he unbuttoned the neck of his shirt, then undid his cuffs and rolled the sleeves to the elbows. His actions increased her nervous tension.

"Nothing for me, thank you."

"Not even Coke?"

"No."

"Then I'll be right back."

The momentary respite didn't give her time to pull herself together because he returned almost instantly with a glass of something alcoholic.

He took a swallow before setting it on top of an end table next to the leather couch, then faced her with his hands in his pockets.

"Since the night you phoned in on the show to announce the open house, I've been talking with my crew, doing a little preliminary research. I've a proposition for you."

Lacey hadn't known what to expect, but certainly she couldn't have guessed it had anything to do with his filmmaking business. "I don't understand."

He stood there with his legs slightly apart, rubbing the back of his neck. "Lorraine's project has caught my imagination. After discussing it with the guys, we've decided we want to do a series of documentaries on the simian aide program from beginning to end.

"We have contacts with major distributors, apart from the NATO foundation, who can push the film on the public in a big way, making a noticeable difference."

At this point Lacey was on her feet. "Are you serious?" she cried, overwhelmed by what he was suggesting.

"Completely. It's for a worthy cause. Just how worthy even I didn't realize until tonight. The tasks required to enhance Ray's life would be tedious and in some ways impossible for a human to stand for any length of time. But George has the capacity to endure the process over and over again. It was very enlightening."

"Lorraine won't believe it. Where will you get the funding?"

His eyes traveled over her, bringing the color to her cheeks. "We have our sources, so that's not a concern. But there is one thing which will require your cooperation, or we won't do it at all." A certain nuance in his voice sent a shiver down her spine.

"You know I'd help any way I can."

A dangerous smile broke the corner of his mouth. "I'm glad you said that because we're going to film the second segment in Florida where the monkeys are held to acclimatize to humans. We need an actress to bring their story to life.

"It must be someone who not only looks great in front of the camera, but is a natural in expressing herself. Since you meet those criterion and have a vested interest in the program, both practically and emotionally, you've been chosen."

"What?" Lacey was aghast.

"That's right. We don't have time to find someone else, and even if we did, we'd never come up with a person who cares the way you do.

"Naturally we're going to want to film some portions of you interacting with George. He's as crazy about you as he is Lorraine, so that won't present any problems."

"But I can't leave my work and go to Florida!"

"Don't you think it's long past time you left Salt Lake for a hard-earned vacation, albeit a working one?" he challenged.

"Max—this isn't a joking matter."

"I heartily agree."

She shook her head. "Even if I could manage to break away, I've never done any acting before. I wouldn't have the faintest idea what to do or say."

"Just be your natural self, the way you were on the program last week. And whatever it is you don't know, the guys can teach you. As far as the script, that's my department. I'll work with Lorraine to get the technical part right." He was moving too fast for her, yet she was thrilled at the idea of going away with him.

"I—I don't have the money to take a long trip anywhere. I'm still paying off the loan on my car."

"Naturally you'll receive a salary and expenses." There was a pause. "However, if you're too wrapped up in your personal life here to see the bigger picture, we'll drop the whole idea." He reached for his drink and swallowed it to the last drop.

Max had a talent for upsetting her, but this time he'd gone too far. "Why are you always making me out to be the villain of the piece? I work hard, just like you. I have commitments, just like you. Why do you repeatedly insinuate that the way I conduct my life is distasteful to you?''

His brows furrowed. ''Distasteful isn't the right word. Let's just say that your lifestyle requires the constant attention of the male of the species. Tonight I couldn't even mention going someplace for dinner without you bringing another man into the conversation. Naturally I can understand why you'd hesitate to give that up.

''Even a week in Florida would probably be too much for you to handle, spent with a man who sees right through you, let alone a crew of married men who won't be taken in by your obvious charms.''

''How dare you say such things to me? How dare you presume to judge me.'' She turned, red-faced, and headed for the back door, but she only made it as far as the kitchen.

''I dare because it's true,'' he muttered, grabbing hold of her shoulders and pulling her back against him with a strength she could hardly countenance. ''Why do you bother to deny it? Men are coming and going from your condo all hours of the day and night.

''I suppose it's addicting, and I should have more sympathy for your problem. It occurred to me that a week in Florida would give you a drying out period which could be a salutary experience.''

She broke free of his arms and whirled around, livid. ''You're crazy, you know that?''

''Then prove me wrong and come to Florida. Show me you can exist without the other men in your life and I just might be convinced.''

Her first instinct was to walk out on him and never

look back. Of course that was exactly what he wanted her to do. Then he could blame her for putting her own selfish needs ahead of Lorraine's, and add that to her growing list of sins.

What perverse streak in his nature had convinced him she couldn't get enough of men? Had someone made up lies about her, lies he believed? Did he mistrust women in general?

Evidently he wanted a woman who was as pure as the driven snow and didn't recognize her when she was right in front of his eyes.

Whatever demons drove him, she'd had enough! That, or fight him at his own game.

Could she? Did she dare?

Much as she wanted to deny it, she cared what Max thought of her. In truth, she'd fallen hopelessly in love with him. She couldn't risk losing him without trying one last time to get to the bottom of his suspicions.

Hardening her resolve, she slowly turned around and looked up at him. "I'll do better than that, Max," she assured him in a husky voice. "I'll give up all men starting right now, provided you give up all the other women in your life, as well. We'll devote ourselves exclusively to each other."

The hands rubbing her upper arms ceased their restless movement. "You mean that?" came the deep query.

"Yes," she answered with her heart in her throat. "Before we leave for Florida, I'd like us to spend all our free time together. I'll fix our meals while you tutor me on the narration.

"Since I've never traveled any long distance, I'm

going to want your advice on what to take, how to get ready. We can shop together. That way we'll never be lonely, and you'll know I'm keeping to my side of the bargain."

A nerve pulsated at the corner of his sensuous mouth, drawing her gaze. "The only way to ensure that promise is to live together. Under the circumstances, I'm going to move in with you tonight."

CHAPTER SEVEN

FOR a minute the room spun. "I—I... You misunderstood my suggestion," she stammered, floundering in water way over her head.

He pierced her with his gaze. "I don't think so. You've just suggested that we share our lives. That means day and night. My constant presence will put an end to wishful thinking on anyone else's part."

Lacey had this suffocating feeling in her chest. No matter how much she wanted to help Lorraine, no matter how desperately she wanted Max's love, she wouldn't sleep with him. In her mind, intimacy of that kind was reserved for marriage.

"Max—before this conversation goes any further, we have to discuss the sleeping arrangements."

An enigmatic smile broke the corner of his mouth. "As I told you before, I'm tempted, but I think we'll both practice abstinence for a while. It's good for the soul. Therefore, you'll sleep in your bed, and I'll make do on the couch."

Surprise and relief washed over her in waves. It appeared he was out to reform her completely. What he didn't know was that she planned to do some reforming of her own, even if it meant going against at least one of her principles and living with a man, living with Max.

"When do you propose to move in?"

"This minute."

"But—"

"But nothing," he replied suavely. "It's called, quitting cold turkey. I'll just gather a few things I need and we'll go home. *Su casa es mi casa.*" He swooped down and kissed her astonished mouth before disappearing from the kitchen.

"I'm out of toothpaste," he called to her from the hallway, "so I'll have to use yours until I can get to the store tomorrow. Come to think of it, I'm low on a lot of things."

While he spoke, Lacey was having an anxiety attack in the middle of his kitchen. She couldn't believe this was happening, or that she was allowing it to happen. His mind moved leap years ahead of hers. She had an idea she might live to regret it.

But when he reappeared moments later with a small duffel bag and slid a possessive arm around her shoulders, drawing her close for another kiss, she practically melted on the spot and found herself walking toward the door with him.

The phone was ringing off the hook as they entered her condo from the back entrance.

"I'll get it," he said, and picked up the receiver on the kitchen wall before she could reach it. His terse hello would have struck terror in the heart of anyone calling.

A scowl confirmed her worst fear. Aside from Lorraine or Valerie, Greg was the only person who phoned her this late at night.

Max muttered something else equally quelling, and hung up the receiver. He turned accusing blue eyes on her. "That was Greg. He said he'd call back in the morning. I thought you told me he had an ex-fiancée."

"He does. They're supposed to be getting married at Christmas, but they had a fight. I'm still hoping they make up."

"How can they do that if he's still calling you late at night?"

"You don't understand." She smoothed a few black curls off her forehead. "Greg grew up across the street from me and Valerie. He's like a brother. My parents took him in after his mother died and his dad moved to New York. We're friends, that's all.

"He drops in on Valerie as much as he does me. But his broken leg has created complications and that's why I've seen more of him than usual."

Max stared at her for endless moments. "Apparently I'm not the only one who finds the time he spends with you suspect."

Because Max had hit upon the one area that had briefly caused trouble in Greg's relationship with Annette, Lacey avoided his scrutiny, suitably chastened.

"At least you haven't attempted to deny it. Under the circumstances, it's a good thing I'm going to be around from here on out. If Greg doesn't learn to lean on his fiancée, their marriage doesn't stand a prayer."

"I agree," she murmured at last, knowing he spoke the truth.

Max made a noise in his throat. "Well, that's something, anyway. Now I don't know about you, but I'm tired. After I call Jeff to get the ball rolling, I'm going to bed.''

Thankful he'd be occupied for the next few minutes, Lacey changed into a nightgown and put on her quilted robe. Then she went in search of linens and blankets.

By the time he was off the phone, she'd made up the couch, a ritual she'd done for Greg on many occasions, but somehow this was different. Her fantasies about Max had, in part, become reality.

''Forget what you're thinking,'' he said when he entered the living room and found her plumping his pillow. She let it go like a hot potato, convinced he had radar to detect her every thought.

''Just so you know, I'm up every morning at six to get ready for work.''

''And I sleep until ten,'' he followed. ''What time do you get home?''

''I never know how long I'll be, but generally it's around four.''

When he started unbuttoning his shirt the rest of the way, she couldn't concentrate and deliberately averted her eyes, but not soon enough to escape his mocking smile.

''I leave for the station at two, which gives us from six-thirty until we both go to bed to be together. I'm off every other Monday and Sunday. With tomorrow being Sunday, we can both sleep in and enjoy a leisurely breakfast.''

''That's fine for you, but I have to get up early enough to prepare my Sunday school lesson. I leave for church at nine-thirty, and don't get home until noon.''

"Then we'll both get up in time to have breakfast together, and I'll go to church with you," he said smoothly.

She fought hard to keep her composure. His image of her didn't include attending church. He didn't believe for a moment she had a class to teach. "Fine."

"I'll even cook our first breakfast so you can work uninterrupted." His heartbreaking smile didn't fool her.

"Then I'll see you in the morning."

"Have a good sleep," he muttered with a devilish gleam in his eye.

"You, too."

The minute she got to her room and shut the door, she hurried to the bedside table to phone Greg and explain why he mustn't drop over whenever he felt like it. But when she picked up the receiver, she couldn't get a dial tone.

After clicking it without success, Lacey decided the phone was off the hook in the kitchen. Had Max done it deliberately? Would he go that far?

She waited half an hour, until she was sure he'd gone to sleep. Then she tiptoed out of her room and down the hall. She had to pass through the living room to get to the kitchen. Fortunately he sounded dead to the world as she quietly padded across the carpet.

"Flattered as I am that you'd like me in your bed tonight, we have an understanding, and there's no way I'm going to let you change the rules."

His voice seemed to come out of nowhere, startling her. "I was going to the kitchen to make me some cocoa."

"If you've never practiced it, self-denial is painful. Actually, I could do with something hot myself." Like lightning, he was on his bare feet and slipped a robe over his striped pajamas.

Lacey groaned as he followed her into the kitchen and turned on the light. Now she'd be forced to fix cocoa when it was the last thing she wanted. Her eyes darted to the wall phone.

"That's right." His gaze followed hers and he flashed her a crooked smile. "I took it off the hook, just to make certain we both get a good night's sleep."

Running a shaky hand through her black curls, she said, "I've changed my mind about a drink." The intimacy of their situation was creating havoc with her senses.

"I thought maybe you would," he taunted. "A couple of aspirins might help you wind down. They're known to have a tranquilizing effect."

"Thank you, *Doctor* Jarvis. Good night."

His chuckle followed her all the way to the bedroom.

When she heard the sound of a doorbell, she thought she must be dreaming, and nestled more comfortably beneath the covers. But the pealing of the bell persisted, and she finally lifted her head from the pillow.

The clock said seven-thirty. Who'd be at her front door this early, on a Sunday morning no less?

She slid out of bed, threw on her robe, and hurried out of her room to answer it. But Max had obviously heard it, as well, and was already making his way to the front door.

No evidence remained of his night on the couch. He must have put his bedding away. Dressed only in the bottom half of his pajamas, his magnificent physique—bronzed like the rest of him—took Lacey's breath.

She could understand the look of complete astonishment on Greg's face when Max opened the door to him. She'd hoped to talk to Greg before something like this could happen, but it was too late now.

"It's Greg, isn't it? Looks like your walking cast is serving you well. What can we do for you?" Max's intimidating voice sounded several registers lower this early in the morning.

Greg's gaze darted to Lacey, who was hovering behind Max. "I didn't meant to intrude. Call me when you get a chance."

"We're up now," Max drawled, making everything that much worse. "Maybe you'd better come in and have your talk with Lacey because we're going to be tied up later."

"It can wait."

"Whatever it is you have to say to Lacey can be said to both of us." Max darted her a melting look and put his arm around her, drawing her to his side in an unmistakable gesture of ownership. "We're living together now."

The color drained out of Greg's face. She knew he'd be shocked because Greg was very much aware of Lacey's moral upbringing and strong religious principles. But she didn't understand the hurt look in his eyes. Max's brief glance in her direction spoke volumes.

"Greg, I—I'm sorry I didn't have a chance to tell you. Why don't you come over for dinner one night next week?"

"No, thanks," he clipped. His face closed up as his gaze flicked to Max.

"I think Lacey's idea is an excellent one," Max said unexpectedly. "I'd like to get to know you better. She says you're practically family. Why not bring your fiancée and make it a foursome? I haven't had a chance to preview the film my crew and I made in the Amazon. Perhaps you and—Annette, is it?— would find it interesting."

"Please come," Lacey begged, sensing Greg's hesitation. She hoped to undo some of the damage. "How about tomorrow night?"

"Monday night happens to be my night off. It's perfect," Max interjected suavely. "Shall we say seven o'clock? You'll be home from work by then, won't you, darling?" He kissed the side of her neck intimately.

For a man who'd only moved in the night before, he'd taken over as if he'd been her husband for a long time. *But that was what she wanted, wasn't it?*

After a pause Greg said, "I'll have to check with Annette."

"You do that, then give us a call. I'll be here, even if Lacey's still working."

Greg mumbled something noncommittal and left.

Max closed the door and locked it. There was an ominous silence. He turned around with a triumphant expression on his face.

"Your family friend has been needing a jolt like that for a long time. I actually felt sorry for the poor devil. But I think he got the point. Maybe now he'll be able to get his act together."

On one level Lacey could hear what he was saying and basically agreed with him. But on another, she was too mesmerized by the sight of his virile, masculine presence to think clearly.

His hair was attractively mussed from sleeping on the couch. The desire to smooth it from his forehead was almost irresistible.

"It's no good looking at me that way," he murmured silkily. "Even if I were amenable to the idea, you've got a Sunday school lesson to get. Remember?"

For a moment she *had* forgotten.

Humiliated that Max could have such a potent effect on her, she dashed into the bathroom to start getting ready. A half hour later, the smell of frying bacon reached her nostrils as she walked into the kitchen dressed in a blouse and skirt, wearing a dark, tailored vest.

"How do you like your eggs?" he called over his shoulder, which was covered by his robe. He looked very much at home, which wasn't surprising since their condos were identical.

"Scrambled."

To her delight he'd set the table and had made orange juice and cinnamon toast of all things. Considering the adventurous life he lived, unencumbered by a wife and family, he could probably take care of himself better than most people.

She couldn't help but wonder how he'd avoided marriage all these years, or more importantly, why. Her spirits plummeted when she realized that their living together wasn't for real. She had no guarantees that the future would bring about a miraculous change in his feelings toward her.

"A little food ought to cheer you up." He placed bacon and eggs in front of her before sitting down to attack his own hearty breakfast.

"Everything's delicious," she said minutes later, discovering she was hungry. "Thank you. No one's fixed me breakfast in years."

"I can understand why." Through veiled eyes he stared at her face and freshly washed black curls. "Food would be the last thing on a man's mind waking up to you in the morning."

She crimsoned at his frank compliment and swallowed her entire glass of juice without taking a breath. "I'm going in the other room to work on my lesson. Leave the dishes and I'll do them after church."

He wiped the corner of his mouth with a napkin. "I think I can manage to clean up and still get ready for church on time." His determination to keep an eye on her was nothing short of amazing.

She thanked him again, then went to the hall closet for her bag. It contained her lesson materials and flannel board. Once she settled down to work, it seemed like she'd barely had time to review the lesson when Max announced he was ready to go.

He must have slipped over to his condo in the interim. He wore a charcoal suit with a pearl-gray shirt and silk tie. Smoothly shaven, he looked devastatingly handsome. Every time she looked at him, her heart pounded out of rhythm.

By tacit agreement they left the condo through her back door and went out to his Saab. This time when he helped her inside, she made sure her skirt covered her knees.

The church she attended was located near the university, a block away from the home where she'd been raised. Her family had gone to services there for as long as she could remember. Everyone knew everyone, and they would all speculate like crazy when they saw her walk in with Max.

Not only would he be the cynosure of every eye, but Lacey had never been to church with anyone outside her family, Greg excepted.

When she suggested that Max go to a meeting for the adults, he said he preferred to watch her teach. With a smile she tried to hide, she told him he might be sorry as she directed him to a roomful of eleven noisy four-year-olds.

They immediately wanted to know all about him and plied him with the usual embarrassing questions like, was he her husband? When were they going to have a baby?

To her surprise, Max handled the children beautifully. One word from him and they settled down to listen to her lesson on being grateful for the growing things around them created by God.

When it came time for them to color their autumn

leaves and cut them out, Max got down on the floor with them. Her throat closed with emotion to see his dark head bent over the pictures with just as much concentration as the children. He was perfectly natural with them and would make a wonderful father.

When it was over, Lacey ushered the children back to their parents who were going into the chapel for the main service.

Max grasped her hand and led her to a pew in the rear. Everyone smiled and nodded, wanting to be introduced to the striking man at her side. In his charismatic way, he charmed everyone, and several people recognized his name as the famous radio personality.

Lacey couldn't hear what went on during the service. All she was aware of was the warmth of Max's hand clasping hers, and the feeling of rightness associated with being here with him. Her heart swelled until she thought it would burst.

As they left the church, Lacey seemed to view the world through new eyes. It was a glorious fall day, the air crisp and clear, the mountains majestic.

"Lacey, honey? Wait a minute. Is this your new beau?" a voice called. It was Mrs. Taggert, an old family friend.

Lacey swung around and hugged her. "This is Max Jarvis, a friend of mine. Max, meet Mrs. Taggert, a dear friend of my parents."

The older woman clucked in delight. "I know who you are. I never miss one of your shows. My eyes are so bad, I have to rely on the radio more and more."

"I'm pleased to hear you enjoy Radio Talk."

"I do now that you're on." She spoke loudly. "It's

about time they brought in someone who has lived in another place besides Utah. We're a little ingrown here, you know.''

Max grinned, his gaze locking with Lacey's. She smiled back. She couldn't help it. For an infinitesimal moment she enjoyed the heady sensation of laughing silently with him over something that was still a bone of contention between them.

''I like Utah,'' he said, directing his attention to the older woman again. ''In fact, I'm thinking of settling down here permanently.''

His admission stunned Lacey. She had no idea his move to Salt had ever been temporary.

Mrs. Taggert beamed. ''Well, you know what Mr. Prentiss said on the radio. The prettiest girls in the world come from Utah.''

''As it happens, I've lived in many parts of the world and I have to agree with you.''

''I tell you—'' She reached for Lacey's arm. ''I like him a lot more than Greg.'' Though she'd said it in a whisper, Max couldn't have helped but hear her.

Greg? Had everyone thought she and Greg were a couple, *except her*? Lacey questioned inwardly.

Deciding to ignore the comment, she said, ''It's nice to see you again, Mrs. Taggert. Now I'm afraid we have to be going.''

They all said their good-byes and Max ushered her to the car. After they'd pulled into the mainstream of traffic he confided, ''I understand more than ever why Greg's fiancée feels less than secure.''

They hadn't been in the car two minutes and already the tension was building.

"Mrs. Taggert has always thought Greg would get together with me or Valerie. But she didn't understand that he was like a brother to us. Neither of us had those kinds of feelings for him."

"On your part, maybe," he conceded, "but Greg definitely has a problem."

"Can we get off the subject of Greg?" she asked heatedly.

"Don't be angry with me because everyone in the world knows Greg is in love with you except you. Between that and your frustration level brought on by deprivation, I think you need a change of scene.

"To show you my heart is in the right place, we'll drive into the mountains and eat dinner along the way. Your lesson has put me in the mood to enjoy the growing things around us."

Inexplicably pleased by his last comment, Lacey relaxed against the seat, opened the window and settled down to enjoy the living, breathing male seated next to her.

Two hours later, after a filling lunch with strawberry pie for dessert, Lacey found herself looking down at Max who'd stretched out next to a mountain stream. The sunshine gilded the blonder highlights of his hair. He was a breathtaking man.

"Now that you know everything about Perry the liar, don't you think it's time I learned why you never married?"

Because his eyes were closed, she thought maybe he hadn't heard her. "Max?" she prompted.

"There've been several women in my life, but the idea of marrying any of them never occurred to me."

She blinked. "Did you live with any of them?"

"No. Only *you* can claim that distinction."

Her heart gave a funny kick. Swallowing hard, she ventured, "Are you saying that you're among that small percentage of men who just aren't interested in being tied down?"

"No. Otherwise I wouldn't be living with you."

Before she knew how it happened, he'd pulled her across the top of him and began kissing her the way she'd been wanting him to do all day.

"But you know what I mean." She gasped the words when he allowed her a breath of air.

Through his lashes, the blue of his eyes had darkened to pitch, and his grip on her was tighter than he probably realized. "Marriage isn't right for everyone. My parents are a living testimony of that fact, but I don't want to talk about them or their divorce. I much prefer enjoying the taste of your strawberry mouth. It's fast becoming my addiction."

Content to have gotten that much information out of him, Lacey nestled closer in his arms, addicted to the very scent and feel of him. Once more she found herself giving him kiss for kiss until she lost complete control.

Max chose that moment to break free of her passionate embrace and stand up. Registering a moan of disappointment, Lacey more or less staggered to her feet. Her body was trembling so hard, she had to cling to him or she would have fallen over.

"All good things have to come to an end," he

whispered before gently biting her earlobe. "Besides, the sun is setting and it's getting cold." He reached for the blanket and her vest, which had somehow come off during their halcyon interlude. Together they walked to the car with their arms around each other's waists.

"I've never seen the mountains this alive with color," she murmured, still filled with a euphoria she'd never known before.

He helped her into the car, then leaned down to kiss her lips as if he couldn't help himself. "I've never seen eyes as green as yours. They defy description." The huskiness in his voice revealed the measure of his entrancement. It was something to hug to herself on the drive back to the condo.

Like clockwork, the phone rang the minute they stepped into her kitchen. Max reached for the phone first, said hello, then proceeded to ask who was calling. After a moment, he put his hand over the receiver.

"It's Cameron Morgan. He's at a convenience store around the corner and wants to know if he can come by tonight to talk to you about a new problem with his accounts."

"Let me speak to him."

Max passed the receiver to her, but stayed planted near the phone.

She turned her back to him, the better to concentrate. When she finally said good-bye, Max replaced the receiver. Judging by the lines marring his features, something was wrong. She couldn't bear it. Not after the joy of this day.

"Before you start in on Cameron," she said, jumping in first, "let's get something straight. Without clients like him, I couldn't make a living. I have to work out of my home, and occasionally I have to conduct business late at night and early in the morning.

"You and I may have an understanding, but if you take exception to the people who've retained me as their CPA, then it will destroy the business I've spent several years building."

The whole time she was talking, he was studying her mouth. Unexpectedly his hands cupped her flushed face. "Now you're the one jumping to conclusions. Even after having you to myself for an entire day, I still don't feel like sharing you with anyone else. But I'll learn to live with it as long as I can do *this* whenever I want."

He lowered his head, seeking and finding her avid mouth until they were once again consumed.

For a minute, Lacey lost cognizance of her surroundings and didn't want to stop what they were doing. It was humiliating to realize that Max was always the one to pull away first.

"When Cameron gets here, I promise to be on my best behavior," he murmured against her mouth.

"Cameron!" He'd be arriving at the condo any second now. "I need to get things ready for him."

"What can I do to help?" Max offered pleasantly, while she was still reeling from the emotions he'd brought to life.

"Stay out of the kitchen while we work," she admonished, dashing to the hall closet for her briefcase.

She heard the doorbell ring as she spread a ledger on the kitchen table.

By the time Max had shown Cameron inside, the two of them were having an amicable discussion. When Max said he'd leave them alone so they could get their work done, Cameron urged him to stay. Max had a way of winning anyone over when he wanted. He made coffee and joined them.

It didn't take long for them to conclude their business. Cameron knew the law well, but he wasn't an accountant, and she'd been able to spot the trouble in a second.

Now that the problem was solved, she was anxious to be alone with Max and got up from the table, expecting Cameron to leave. To her surprise, Max had engaged him in conversation, and the two of them more or less ignored her.

Feeling left out because she'd had Max's exclusive attention for the last twenty-four hours, she went into the other room and turned on the TV. When she'd told Max to be nice to her clients, she hadn't expected him to go this far.

By the time Cameron thanked her for her outstanding work and said good-night, she was practically asleep on the couch. Max saw him out, then locked up and turned off the TV.

"Time to go to your own bed, sleepyhead."

"Not yet."

"Up you come." After brushing her lips provocatively with his own, he scooped her into his arms and carried her to the bedroom, depositing her on the queen-size bed.

Her green eyes opened and she stared at him through sooty black lashes. She wanted to tell him what this day had meant to her. "Max—"

A tremor shook his powerful body. "Go to sleep, Lacey." Suddenly the room went black and she heard the door click.

CHAPTER EIGHT

LACEY could smell coffee while she was getting ready for work the next morning. She thought Max would sleep till ten, but was glad he was up because she was so much in love, she didn't want to miss out on a single moment with him.

Last night he'd shown amazing self-control when he'd put her to bed. More than she had...

"Good morning." He greeted her with a melting smile as she walked into the kitchen. To her surprise he was dressed in a T-shirt and Levi's, reading the morning paper while he drank the hot brew. "Your breakfast is in the oven staying warm."

"You shouldn't have gone to the trouble, but I'm glad you did. I've been wanting to talk to you about yesterday."

"I know what you're going to say," he interrupted her, putting down the paper. "It was a good day for me, too. We'll do it again soon."

Happiness filled her to overflowing. "Promise?"

He favored her with one of his penetrating glances. "Come here, Lacey."

Something in his voice sent her heart tripping over itself. She closed the expanse between them and was pulled onto his lap. His mouth closed over hers and they clung to each other in a long, deeply satisfying kiss.

"Um...this morning you taste of mint. What a shame you have to go to work," he murmured before putting her gently but firmly away from him to pour himself another cup of coffee.

As usual, he'd been the one to bring their kiss to an end. Flushed and out of breath, Lacey reached in the oven for her breakfast. Bacon and pancakes. He was spoiling her rotten and she'd never been so happy in her life.

The trick was to overwhelm him with so much love, he'd propose marriage and they could live this way forever. But first, she had to win his complete trust.

After eating everything on her plate and thanking him for the delicious breakfast, she went over to the end of the counter where she kept pad and pencil.

"I'm making you a list of all the places and phone numbers where I'll be today in case you need to get in touch with me. I realize we could be having company tonight, but I'm afraid I won't be home much before six. Dr. Gerard is fitting me in at the end of the day for the last in a series of hepatitis shots Lorraine had me start before I began tending George. I'm writing down his number, as well."

"Don't worry about Greg and Annette," Max inserted. "If they decide to come over, I'll take care of dinner. When you get home from work, you won't have to lift a finger."

Yes! Her plan to keep him informed of her every move was off to a perfect start.

Acting on a burst of heady emotion, Lacey walked back to the table where he was sitting and wrapped her arms around his neck. "Thank you for being so wonderful," she whispered against the side of his jaw.

At first she didn't understand when Max got abruptly to his feet. That is until she caught the fleeting glimpse of desire igniting his eyes before they were hidden by shuttered lids.

In his effort to reform her, it seemed he'd forgotten about his own needs. The knowledge that he wasn't as in control as he would have Lacey believe, filled her with elation.

"What are your plans today?" she asked quietly.

"Jeff's coming over in a few minutes for an initial planning session."

"That sounds exciting. When I'm not at work, I'll do everything I can to help, too. Thanks to your generosity and humanitarianism, a once-in-a-lifetime opportunity has come my way to pay back Lorraine."

"I would think tending George went a long way toward settling your debt with her."

Lacey grinned. "You're right. Now I need to make reparations to a certain male neighbor of mine who was kept awake nights by George's antics."

One dark blond brow quirked rakishly. "Kept awake doesn't quite cover it."

A low chuckle rippled out of Lacey. "I can see that I'd better get going." *The only problem was, she didn't want to go anywhere. She wanted to stay home and play house with Max.*

Apparently he wanted the same thing. Halfway out the back door to her car, two strong hands grabbed her hips and she was spun around.

"I want a good-bye kiss."

"Whatever you say," came her breathless response, eagerly meeting the masculine mouth descending on hers.

But at the first moment of contact, all playfulness fled. As if she had a fire in her veins, Lacey clung to him, burning up with need, a need he was reciprocating with an intensity to equal her own.

Somewhere in the periphery she heard the front doorbell ring. This was followed by a smothered groan from Max, who released her so fast she had to brace herself against the door jamb to recover before going out to the car.

She rested her head against the steering wheel before starting up the motor. Whatever Max had intended, that kiss was no good-bye kiss. It was alive with the promise of all the things he couldn't say to her yet.

One day, Max Jarvis. One day...

Lacey's day started out with no problems until she made an unscheduled stop at noon to see how Greg was doing, and find out if he was back with Annette.

The second they were alone, he chastised her for living with Max, then demanded to know if she was in love with him.

Though Lacey feared her love for Max would never be reciprocated, she answered 'yes' to Greg's question with her usual forthright honesty.

After a sustained silence, she heard him mutter that he wouldn't be coming over for dinner with Annette, so not to expect them. Lacey said she was sorry they

couldn't make it, but that she and Max would invite
them again soon. Greg promptly told her to forget it.

Since he was in such a bad mood, she didn't follow
through with her plan to treat him to a hamburger.
Instead, she ate lunch by herself, then went to her next
appointment and worked steadily until it was time to
go to the doctor's office. Fortunately the reception
room was empty and it only took a matter of seconds
to receive her shot.

By that time, she could hardly wait to get home to
Max.

*How had she lived this long without him? What
would it be like to go home to an empty apartment
now? She couldn't comprehend it, not since he'd
moved in.*

She'd been remembering the kiss they'd shared before she'd gotten in her car that morning, and was
living for a repeat performance.

"Max?" she cried breathlessly, letting herself in
the back door. Dinner was in progress, but he was
nowhere in sight. In her eagerness to see him, she
plopped her briefcase on the floor and went running
into the other room, calling his name.

"I'm right here," he murmured, his head bent over
the desk where he'd obviously been working on a
script for the documentary.

Somehow Lacey had envisioned any other welcome
than this one and her spirits deflated in an instant. He
didn't look at her, let alone get up.

"You've had several calls, among them one from
Valerie."

She mouthed her sister's name in puzzlement.

"That's odd. Valerie never phones this time of day. Did she say what was wrong?"

Suddenly he pushed himself away from the desk and stood up, submitting her to a cold, silent scrutiny. Gone was the loverlike man who'd had trouble letting her out of his arms before she'd left for work nine hours earlier.

"It seems after you visited Greg's office at lunch, he called Valerie very upset. He told her we were living together. She wanted to know if it was true."

Lacey's eyes closed tightly. Before leaving the condo, she'd made out her daily schedule for Max, expressly to show him she could be trusted. Within three hours, she'd proved that she was a liar, and shivered because he would never forgive her for not telling him about her stop to Greg's office.

Aside from the fact that Greg had no right to say anything at all, Lacey had wanted to discuss certain developments with Valerie in her own good time. Now everything had blown up in her face and she had no one to blame but herself.

"W-what did you tell her?" she stammered.

"Actually it was more a case of her congratulating me after I answered the phone."

"Congratulating?"

"It seems she's been worried about you since the Perry episode and is overjoyed to learn that you've finally come out of your shell. She is still under the illusion that you are an innocent."

His words devastated Lacey. An unintentional mistake had put them back to square one. "Max— It was a spontaneous idea on my part because his office is so close to Croft's. I decided to stop by and see if he and Annette were coming for dinner.''

"Did you honestly think he'd consider it?" His voice grated.

"I hoped. We've been friends since we were kids. I'd hate to see it end with such hard feelings."

She couldn't decipher his closed expression. "Your sister doesn't seem to be worried about it. In so many words, she gave us her blessing and is thrilled you're going to Florida with me, particularly as you've never been anywhere except California." After a pause, he added, "She asked me to take good care of you."

Lacey couldn't sustain his glance and lowered her eyes. "What did you say to that?"

"I told her I'd guard you with my life."

It almost sounded like a threat.

Lacey couldn't stand it any longer. "Maybe you should hear the underlying reason why I went to see Greg." Her voice shook.

His brow quirked. "*Underlying reason?*"

Throwing caution to the wind, she lifted her head and stared into his eyes. "I told him t-that I was in love with you," she blurted, causing the room to reverberate with her unequivocal declaration.

Max stared back for several soul-destroying moments. "No wonder he phoned Valerie."

The tight bands around her chest relaxed a little. "I wanted to be certain he understood that I could never live with a man unless I loved him beyond anything in existence. He has suspected my feelings about you from the beginning, but I guess hearing the words drove him to make that call."

After another tension-fraught silence she thought she heard him whisper her name, but the sound of the doorbell intruded on their privacy.

"That'll be the crew," he murmured.

Lacey could have cried aloud her disappointment. Right now the only thing she wanted was to be in his arms and hear him tell her he loved her, too, but that was impossible.

After discovering that she'd gone to Greg's office, he'd apparently made a last-minute decision to fill the house with people. Not only hadn't he wanted to be alone with her, he'd seen no need to consult her.

No matter what she said or did, she couldn't seem to do it right where he was concerned and feared this was an unbreakable pattern. Admitting that she was in love with him was probably the worst thing she could have done. Now he would have the ultimate weapon to use against her.

"I have to freshen up," she said in a quiet voice, and hurried from the room, but he followed her despite the loud knocking at the front door.

In thick tones he said, "Whatever you're thinking, you'd be wrong, but now isn't the time to discuss it. I thought you should know that I included Lorraine in tonight's invitation."

Not Lorraine, she moaned inwardly as he disappeared from the hallway leading to her bedroom. Since he'd invited the older woman to come over before Lacey could explain about Max moving in with her, she was distinctly uncomfortable. Though Lorraine would never pass judgment, Lacey wanted her to know the real truth.

But Lacey never found the opportunity. As soon as Max introduced Lorraine to the crew, he explained how he wished to proceed with the documentary. While they ate, Lorraine gave them background information and suggestions.

Lacey tried, but she couldn't concentrate very well. As soon as the others went home, she'd be alone with Max and wondered what it was he had to say to her.

Aside from the actual filmmaking, each member of the crew had designated responsibilities for working in the field. To Lacey, it sounded like an enormous undertaking. She couldn't imagine doing the job they expected of her. At one point she suggested that Lorraine be the one to act the part.

Lorraine laughed as if the idea were preposterous, and explained that she could never leave while she was in the process of helping George adapt to his new patient. The first few months of bonding were critical.

Adding her voice to the others, Lorraine told Lacey she was the perfect person to play the part of a psychologist. She also brought up the point that as Lacey was self-employed, she could arrange to be gone for the anticipated two weeks. Her words effectively cut off further argument.

Milo, more than the others, seemed sensitive to Lacey's mood and managed to engage her in conversation. A serious type by nature, he was probably the oldest of the four men, closer to forty. Max had told her he was married, but Milo didn't mention his spouse.

Of the three friends, Lacey liked Milo best. He

seemed to enjoy a good, philosophical discussion as much as she did, yet remained mellow.

As far as she could tell, the four men were compatible and loved their work. If they had opinions about her relationship with Max, they didn't express them. Certainly by now they'd have been informed that he'd moved in with her.

Several times throughout the evening she'd felt Max's gaze on her, but when she looked up, he'd be talking to someone else. When everyone started to leave, her heart pounded out of rhythm. In a few minutes she'd be alone with him. As she gave Lorraine a hug and saw her out the door, fear and excitement warred inside of her.

"Lacey?"

With her heart in her throat, she whirled around to discover him standing in the doorway between the kitchen and the living room.

"Charlie Albright called the condo before you came home. He's too sick to do the twelve-to-four shift and asked me to fill in for him. I've got to leave now. Forget the dishes. I'll do them tomorrow."

He couldn't leave now.

She bit her underlip so hard it drew blood. "Do you feel like company?"

"You're always welcome as a guest on Radio Talk, but considering the heavy workload ahead of you to get ready for our trip, don't you think it unwise to stay up all night, too?"

He was saying one thing and meaning another. It was clear to Lacey that he didn't want to be alone with her. Obviously he hadn't believed her avowal of love, or else it had made him claustrophobic.

What had he said about never having entertained the thought of marriage? Though he wanted a relationship with her, he wasn't in the market for a wife and didn't want her to hold out any false hope.

Since they weren't sleeping together, she couldn't figure out what he was getting from their unorthodox arrangement. Nothing made sense. She almost preferred his anger to this polite, civilized stranger he'd become since she'd declared her love. *Never again.*

"You're right. I'm exhausted and my arm is starting to ache. See you tomorrow."

His eyes were half shuttered. "I'll lock up."

"Thanks."

She heard his key turn the dead bolt of the back door. The second he revved the Saab's motor, she rushed into the kitchen and placed a call to Valerie.

"Answer it," she prayed, needing her sister as she'd never needed her before.

A half hour later, a drained Lacey hung up the receiver wondering if she'd be able to take Valerie's advice. Her sister agreed that Max's behavior was too bizarre to put up with much longer, particularly since Lacey had foregone her pride and told him she loved him. But since she'd be leaving with Max for Florida in a week's time, it would be best to go along with things until the film had been made.

If by then Max still hadn't explained himself, then it was time for Lacey to say good-bye and get on with the rest of her life.

"*What life?*" she cried to the empty room, loading

the dishwasher without thinking what she was doing. A pain too deep for tears seared her insides. This wasn't like the Perry incident. Lacey lived with the very real fear that Max had ruined her forever…

The next week proved to be her worst nightmare. She saw very little of Max, who spent most of his free time with the crew. When he was home, he urged her to study her lines, but never brought up anything personal or detained her with the kind of smoldering kisses she ached for.

He still continued to cook their dinner, but more often than not she came home to an empty house after work and ate alone.

The day before the trip, Lacey cleaned the condo from top to bottom. Of necessity, Max left early for his condo to attend to his packing and personal business. For the first time in weeks she had the place to herself. But despite the precarious state of affairs between them, within five minutes she was mourning his absence. By afternoon she'd worked herself into a crisis state because she loved him so desperately and couldn't fathom life without him.

Lorraine's phone call forced Lacey to pull herself together and pretend everything was wonderful. The older woman volunteered to check both Max's and Lacey's condos every day, water plants and see to the mail. She said it was the least she could do while they were gone, which relieved one of Lacey's worries. But nothing could take away her fear that when they returned from Florida, she'd never see Max again.

As the dinner hour approached, she sent out for

pizza, expecting he would make an appearance, but there was no sign of him. He'd gone off someplace in his car.

She lost her appetite completely and went into the bedroom to finish her packing. Around nine the doorbell rang.

Praying it was Max, she dashed into the living room. Occasionally he parked in front and let himself in with the key. But he couldn't gain entrance until she undid the dead bolt.

"Max?" she cried with breathless excitement and flung open the door. She felt like he'd been gone twelve years instead of twelve hours.

"Sorry," Greg said in a quiet voice. He stood there, still wearing his walking cast.

Lacey fought to mask her disappointment. "Are you coming as friend or foe?"

"I just wanted to say good-bye and give you a little going-away present."

"For heaven's sake, Greg! Come in and stop acting as if we'd only met yesterday."

After a slight hesitation, he entered the condo but didn't sit down. "How soon do you expect the lord of the manor?"

She closed the door behind him. "I have no idea."

"That's surprising, considering neither of you has budged from the nest for days."

"You'd have been welcome any time and you know it."

"With Max Jarvis hanging on my every word? No thanks."

Lacey let out a deep sigh. "Greg? Why are you behaving like this? Where has my brother gone?"

His face blanched. "You never could see me, could you, Lacey?"

There was no point in pretending she'd misunderstood him. "You were the brother Valerie and I always wanted."

"You were the girl I always wanted."

"I'm sorry, Greg. I had no idea you felt that way."

His lips thinned. "Are you going to marry him?"

Her heart plummeted to her feet. "I can't answer that question right now. What about Annette?"

"It's no good."

"I don't believe that. You're upset because the relationship you and I've shared over the years has changed. It was bound to change, Greg. For both of us. We couldn't go on existing as we did when we were kids. I think you're feeling possessive of me, and have confused this feeling with love. They aren't the same thing."

He appeared to ponder her comments for a minute, then reached into his pocket and pulled out a present. "Here."

Lacey took the tiny gift-wrapped box from him and opened it. Inside was a green jeweled pin of a monkey. She lifted her head in consternation. "How much—"

"The cost isn't important. When I saw it, the face reminded me of George and I felt like buying it as a peace offering."

"I love it! As far as I'm concerned, we'll always be best friends. Thank you," she said, and gave him a friendly hug which, after a moment's hesitation, he reciprocated.

"What a touching scene," a voice of pure ice resounded in the room.

Lacey spun away guiltily from Greg. Neither of them had heard Max come in through the back door. She could imagine what was running through his mind. The minute his back was turned, she was in Greg's arms. But in his black mood, he'd never believe her explanation, so why try to defend herself.

"Your dinner is in the oven if you want some."

His eyes glinted like metallic shards. "How thoughtful of you, considering you've been occupied elsewhere." The insinuation was unmistakable.

"I dropped in to give Lacey a going-away present," Greg interjected.

Lacey held her breath as Max strolled toward her and put a possessive arm around her shoulders, the first physical contact they'd had in a week. He plucked the pin from her trembling hand and examined it.

"That's a nice piece of jewelry. I wish I'd found it first. The stones are the exact green of your eyes, sweetheart."

He'd never called her *sweetheart* before. It meant he'd passed from being angry to furious.

Greg must have read the signs because he said, "You're a lucky man, Jarvis. Lacey's the best. Have a great trip and come home safely." He disappeared out the front door before she could say good-bye.

At that moment Lacey admired Greg more than at any other time in their lives. The fact that he was finally letting go of a fantasy proved that he was growing up. It took courage to do that in front of Max, and she said as much to him.

"I agree." His tone was glacial. He drew her against him roughly, causing the pin to drop to the floor, but he paid no attention. "Particularly as I don't know if you *are* the best. I'm probably the only man of your acquaintance who hasn't sampled the goods."

Suddenly his mouth was covering hers with smothering force. He crushed her in his arms and held her so tightly, their heartbeats merged. It wasn't as much a kiss as a punishment. Lacey fought for air. "Max!" she gasped in protest.

With his chest heaving he demanded, "How long has he been over here?"

"Not long enough to do what your fertile imagination has envisioned." She lashed out in a rage. "For your information, he's come to accept the fact that I'm in love with *you!*"

With features devoid of expression, he slowly lifted his hand and caressed her silky throat with his fingers. "That's the second time I've heard you say that. Do you know—" his voice rasped "—fool that I am, I was halfway beginning to believe you were capable of that elusive emotion until I walked in here tonight?"

Beneath the anger she thought she detected pain.

One hot tear spilled down her cheek. "So what are you saying? Because of what you *think* was going on in your absence, you're calling off the project?" she cried bitterly, her eyes deep green pools of anguish.

"No," he muttered gruffly. "It's too late for that.

We're going ahead as scheduled with one slight hitch in plans. I want nothing more to do with you, so you'll be on your own from here on out. I'll bunk with Nick. You can do your thing with any male who crosses your path, but leave my crew alone. The minute I see you causing trouble, you'll be sent home so fast you won't know what happened."

He released her with enough force that she had to grab hold of the nearest chair to keep from falling.

"Max—" she called after him, desperate to make him understand. But he was gone. When the door slammed shut, she had the awful premonition he would never willingly walk through it again.

CHAPTER NINE

INSTEAD of being rested for the long flight to Miami, Lacey was white-faced from lack of sleep and puffy-eyed when the taxi pulled up in front of the condo the next morning as planned.

After ringing her front doorbell, Max took her bags out to the taxi. He didn't look at her or say as much as a good morning. An uncomfortable silence pervaded the taxi's interior all the way to Salt Lake International Airport.

Under the circumstances, Lacey greeted Milo with warm enthusiasm when they reached the lounge. If Max intended to freeze her out, at least she had Milo to talk to. Nick and Jeff had already left the day before with their families and would meet them in Miami.

Lacey had a hard time believing this day had come. If only Max would be kind, she could enjoy her first trip in years. As it was, she felt nervous and keyed up.

To make matters worse, Max discussed business with Milo most of the way to Florida. When they met up with the others in Miami and piled into the van for the trip to a beachfront hotel, Max made sure he didn't sit by her. The crew obviously knew something was wrong, but kept quiet about it, which didn't augur well for a good beginning.

148

Jeff had made all the travel arrangements and handed her the room key which should have been Max's. For a brief moment, Jeff's eyes met hers in a silent message of commiseration before she followed the bellboy to the elevator. Of necessity, she had to pass Max, who was deep in conversation with Milo and didn't appear to notice her departure.

Their plan was to meet in the hotel dining room for a late supper, then go to bed. In the morning, they'd drive a large rental van to the Everglades.

A tiny village just outside the borders of the Everglades Park would be their home for the next ten days. Apparently it was nothing more than a compound run by employees of the Florida Simian Society where the monkeys were brought from South America.

After Max's treatment of her, the thought of food made Lacey slightly nauseated. Since she craved sleep and couldn't bear the thought of being in his taciturn presence a second longer than necessary, she called room service and asked that soup and salad be sent up.

Later, while she was eating, there was a rap on her door. "Lacey?" Max called peremptorily. "Why aren't you downstairs with the rest of us?"

She cleared her throat. "I'm exhausted and decided to eat dinner in my room. After a good night's sleep, I'll be ready to go in the morning. Eight o'clock in the lobby, right?"

He muttered something she couldn't understand and went away, much to her relief.

By seven the next morning, Lacey had showered

and dressed in lightweight cotton pants and blouse. The tan safari-style outfit was comfortable, but accentuated her prominent curves. With a sigh, she packed her overnight bag and went down to the lobby to leave it with reception.

Since she'd slept better than she'd anticipated, she found she was hungry and strode into the nearly empty dining room decorated with exotic flowering plants of all types. It was a veritable Garden of Eden.

To her chagrin, she managed to capture the attention of every dark-eyed male waiter in the room. They rushed to take her order, then broke into rapid Spanish, making it impossible to understand very much, even though she'd taken language in school.

Each of them came by her table on one pretext or other. Toward the end of her meal, five or six of them congregated around, wreathed in smiles, plying her with questions in English. How long was she staying? Could they show her around when they went off duty?

After Max's hostility, their harmless attention was balm to her soul. It felt good to laugh and not have to feel on her guard every second.

"In case you're in danger of forgetting the reason why we're here, the guys are waiting in the lobby."

Max's menacing voice sent the young waiters scattering in all directions.

At his high-handed attitude, Lacey's facial muscles constricted, and she glanced at her watch. It was only ten to eight!

She'd taken all the abuse she could stand and turned to tell him so, but the words died on her lips.

Dressed in a khaki shirt similar to hers, and a pair

of hip-hugging jeans, his masculinity reached out to her like a living thing.

Yet his expression was uncompromising, and his bronzed complexion had a definite pallor, as if he hadn't slept well. Even more disturbing was the way his eyes swept over her body in frank appraisal, making her tremble with unassuaged longing.

While he dealt with the bill she asked, "Aren't any of you going to eat before we leave?"

He encircled her wrist with his hand and ushered her from the dining room. "If you had joined us last evening, you would have known we planned to have breakfast at six-thirty."

The crew's enthusiastic greeting prevented further chastisement. They were ready to go. Their flattering comments about her looks sustained her all the way out to the huge rental van. Surprisingly enough, Max shared a seat with her, but neither of them said a word.

The afternoon before, Lacey had been too drained to take cognizance of her surroundings. This morning she determined to ignore Max and enjoy the scenery.

After living in the Rocky Mountains, the flatness of the land made a huge impact, as did the tall buildings of steel and smoked glass.

Billboards and fast-food restaurants crammed the highway leading to the Everglades. Soon they were surrounded by prairie, swampland and cabbage palms. She'd read the book, *River of Grass*, in preparation for her trip and marveled at the vegetation which could only grow in such a warm, humid climate.

They passed a small Miccosukee village displaying

Native artifacts and her excitement grew. "Max—" she whispered tentatively, "please let's try to get along while we're here and not let what's wrong affect the others."

"If that's an invitation for me to join you in your hut, think again."

His low, unexpected reply stung and succeeded in silencing her for the rest of the drive to the compound hidden deep in foliage she couldn't begin to identify.

The moment the van drew up to the main building, Max jumped out. Milo happened to be the person closest to Lacey and clasped her slender waist to help her get down. It was a gesture that didn't escape Max's notice, judging from his tight-lipped grimace. He was standing a few yards off, separating the luggage and camera equipment.

Jeff drew close to her. "Your hut is next to the main building. Follow the trail." A well-traveled footpath disappeared into the alien green world surrounding them.

Suddenly she was aware of Max's eyes fastened on her with an intimacy that sent her pulse racing. The cloying humidity had caused her clothes to mold to the lines and curves of her body like a second skin and there was absolutely nothing she could do about it.

Right now she felt as if they were the only two people in the world. If that were the case, maybe then he'd put away his suspicions and love her.

"I can carry my own bags."

Max shook his head, drawing her attention to his dark blond hair, which had a tendency to curl in the moist heat. "You need to take it easy for the rest of the day and acclimatize first. We won't start filming until tomorrow."

As they started along the path, a woman close to Lorraine's age with gray-blond hair hurried toward them dressed in jeans and a blouse. Her mouth broke into a broad smile when she saw them.

"We've been waiting for you to come. Any interest in the simian aide program is welcomed. I'm Ruth Stevens."

Max shook her hand and said, "Ruth, this is Lacey West. She'll be starring in our documentary."

She pumped Lacey's hand. "We're thrilled to have you, Lacey. In fact, we're just one big happy family around here and eat our meals together in the compound dining room. No one stands on ceremony."

"It sounds wonderful," Lacey commented, liking Ruth immediately. "What are your responsibilities?"

"Professionally, I'm a veterinarian. Personally, I take care of my husband, Drew, who has been studying simians for years and created the institute."

"You make me feel as if I'm doing absolutely nothing with my life."

"I wouldn't call making a film to help the other-abled, nothing. It's a tremendously significant program." Her gaze darted from Lacey to Max. "Drew is impressed that someone of your international reputation would choose to make this kind of contribution, Mr. Jarvis."

"Max," he interjected with a genuine smile that robbed Lacey of breath.

"Max." The older woman beamed back. "Drew

wants you to know he's pledged his full support while you're here.''

"We're grateful for your cooperation and will try to do the project justice. But in all honesty, if it weren't for Lacey, who introduced me to a trained monkey named George, I would never have known about the program or the good it can do. Her dedication to the cause is the reason we're here.''

Giving Lacey credit for the project should have warmed her heart, but there was too much enmity between them. His cruelty had hurt her to the point of numbness.

Lacey continued to follow Ruth with Max trailing a few steps behind until they came to a wood hut nestled in the verdure.

"There's plenty of room for everybody. Lacey, I've put you here because it's closest to the main building where Drew and I live. At first, the noises at night are a little unnerving. If you feel like company, you can run over. The door is never locked.''

"Thank you,'' she said, touched by the older woman's concern.

"Max— I understand you'll be rooming with one of your crew. It looks as if Drew has already shown them their quarters. Go ahead and make yourselves comfortable, then come over to the main hut. That's where the rest room and showers are located. I have fresh, icy-cold lemonade waiting.''

"That sounds divine,'' Lacey murmured. "Thank you for the warm welcome. You've made me feel perfectly at home.''

Ruth put her hands on her hips. "Well, it may not

be what you're used to, but we have all the necessary comforts. I'll see you in a while.''

As Ruth walked off, Lacey entered her own designated hut, aware of Max at her heels. They entered the square room bungalow and he put her bags on the floor.

Her gaze wandered from the cot with its mosquito netting to the dresser and wardrobe. Woven mats of a beautiful Native design covered the floor, and flowered curtains hung at the small windows. Everything was spotlessly clean. She couldn't have asked for more.

Max's expression was inscrutable. ''Just so you know, I'll be rooming with Milo in the cabin next to this one.''

Her proud chin lifted. ''I'm surprised you'd put yourself in the path of temptation, or is it that you have a perverted need to monitor my nocturnal activities?''

His eyes narrowed to slits. ''Actually I thought you'd be comforted to know help was at hand in case a predator or something equally deadly invaded your chambers during the night.''

''Knowing how your mind works, you're praying it will happen. Anything to disturb my clandestine assignations. But I have news for you. I don't frighten easily.'' The lie rolled off her lips.

He'd just painted pictures that made her shudder in horror. She made up her mind then and there that if anything untoward *did* happen, he'd be the last person to whom she'd appeal for help.

''We'll see, won't we,'' he mocked, and walked out

on her, closing the door quietly behind him. In a rage, she threw herself on the cot.

Lacey had heard of women and men who fought physically with each other, but could never imagine such a thing happening...until she'd met Max whose attitude was so impossible, she'd come close to slapping his face. Whoever said the line between love and hate was almost indistinguishable, must have known Max Jarvis!

The cot felt good. In her lethargy, brought on by the humidity, she slept for a while and awakened an hour later feeling a little better, but terribly thirsty.

Gathering up a few essentials, she headed for the main hut, which turned out to be a rectangular building made of wood like the other huts. She could hear a generator going, evidence of modern technology in a world which had been here since the beginning of time.

As soon as she stepped inside the hallway, a male voice said hello. Lacey turned her head in time to see a good-looking Hispanic man about her age exiting the dining room.

"You must be the actress Ruth was telling us about. I'm Carlos Rivera, and this is my first job as a veterinarian."

"I'm Lacey West, a CPA from Salt Lake City."

His white smile deepened. "Brains and beauty. Will you join me for a drink?"

"I'd like that. Just give me five minutes."

The bathroom was surprisingly modern and sanitary. She washed her face and gave her curls a good brushing. After putting on fresh lip gloss, she felt slightly more human as she went in search of Carlos.

The dining room cum lounge contained chairs, a large couch and several bookshelves holding every conceivable type of reading material as well as a variety of puzzles and games. On the other side was a large rectangular table and hutch.

"There you are." Ruth came from the direction of the kitchen, holding out drinks for both of them. "I was almost about to come and get you."

"The heat is enervating, so I took a nap." She drank a long swallow of lemonade and thought nothing had ever tasted so delicious.

"Good for you," Carlos chimed in. "The first day you must do nothing but play."

"Carlos? Why not take Lacey to the pool this afternoon? The lagoon is the best place I know to relax and cool off. I sent Max and the others there over an hour ago."

At the mention of Max's name, Lacey's breathing constricted. "Maybe later."

All she needed was for Max to catch her swimming with Carlos. No matter how much she was tempted to flaunt the young vet in Max's face, she knew it would backfire on her.

The crew was here to do a documentary. Since they'd be working nonstop for the next ten days, and cooperation was essential, she had no desire to escalate their personal war.

Carlos eyed her intently. "Perhaps you'd like to visit the animal hospital where the monkeys are housed."

"I'd love it," she enthused. Max couldn't find fault with her for touring the facility.

Ruth took their empty glasses. "By the time you're back, dinner will be ready."

For the next two hours, Lacey became completely engrossed as Carlos showed her the amazing laboratory she would never have dreamed existed here. Beyond it, over a dozen capuchin monkeys were enclosed in a huge, open-air cage covering a half acre of ground which replicated their habitat.

The monkeys reminded her so much of George, she felt right at home. Carlos was an expert on simians. He explained that not all monkeys made good companions, particularly those who came into the program with questionable backgrounds.

He also indicated that the program didn't work for every other-abled person. Now Lacey understood why Lorraine was so adamant about training monkeys from birth. Lacey's eyes were opened to the complexity of the situation and Carlos's reasoning gave her a lot to mull over as they walked back to the lounge.

Deep in concentration with him, she didn't realize they were the focus of attention until she felt Max's accusing gaze as they entered the dining room.

"There you are," Ruth called from the kitchen. "I've been keeping your food hot."

"I'm afraid we lost track of the time," Carlos offered to no one in particular.

Ruth's husband got to his feet. He was a tall man with a nasty scar down the side of his jaw and throat. "We haven't met yet. I'm Drew Stevens."

Lacey shook his outstretched hand. "I'm Lacey West. How do you do?"

He kept on holding it and gave her a warm smile before his gaze flicked to Carlos. "I'd say we're doing just fine. What do you think about our place?"

"It's incredible. Fascinating. I still can't believe I'm here."

"Ruth and I know exactly what you mean," he said kindly, and let go of her hand. "We came out here thirty-six years ago and have never left. Have a seat. Ruth has cooked a special chicken dinner in your honor."

Lacey needed no further inducement and took her place next to Drew. Dinner was a lively affair with the Stevenses and Carlos entertaining everyone's questions. But when eight o'clock rolled around, Max announced it was time for bed. Night fell quickly in the Glades, and they'd begin filming at six the next morning. The crew needed to get their sleep.

"I'll walk you to your hut," Max asserted just as Carlos urged Lacey to stay and talk for a while. "There's a slight change in the script I need to discuss with you before we begin tomorrow's shoot."

Lacey's eyes closed involuntarily at the dreaded inquisition she'd have to face once she was alone with Max. With a murmur of regret to Carlos, and a sincere thank you to the Stevenses for everything, she followed Max and the others out of the lounge.

To her astonishment, he didn't say a word about Carlos as he used a flashlight to guide them to her hut. Once there, he flicked on the electricity.

"This afternoon we scouted around for possible

spots to begin shooting, and felt the pool is the best place to start. The melaleuca trees overhead are filled with black wingers and kites. We also discovered a family of snowy egrets. The setting is exotic and the light is right. It gave me an idea for the opening. I've done a rough draft and have left it on your dresser. I want you to study it before you go to bed.''

Right now Max was the total professional. All his pent-up anger seemed to be missing. When he was like this, she ached for the closeness and intimacy they'd once shared. When he turned to leave, she caught hold of his arm. Immediately, his whole demeanor altered.

Pained by his reaction, she quickly let go. ''Max— I wouldn't presume to tell you how to do your work, but this afternoon when Dr. Rivera was showing me the sick monkeys in the lab, he gave me some new insights into the reason why the monkeys are so expensive.

''It occurred to me you might want to feature him in the film, using the lab for a backdrop. It was an enlightening two hours.''

Max was silent so long, she thought he hadn't heard her. Or worse, that he'd mock the idea because she'd suggested using the only eligible, available male around.

Again he surprised her by saying, ''Why don't you reconstruct your conversation for me right now and I'll work on a draft tonight. No doubt Rivera will bend over backward to oblige as long as you're the co-star. I'll get my notebook.''

She stared at his retreating back with despair. Every

time she thought she was making progress, Max attacked with some cutting remark that knocked the foundations out from under her. She was fast losing hope he'd ever fall in love with her.

Momentarily he returned and pulled a chair close to the cot. His lithe movements drew her gaze as he stretched his muscular legs in front of him. The dim light from the ceiling threw his rugged features into stark relief. This close, she craved his touch, his smile, one tender look.

At his bidding, she sat down on the bed and tried to remember exactly what had been said back in the lab. But as he wrote, her attention fastened on his luxuriant hair. The humidity caused it to curl around his forehead and neck. She had an irresistible urge to play with it.

Her eyes drifted over his intelligent face and dwelled on the firm mouth which had lit a fire the first time he'd kissed her. No matter how horribly he treated her, she wanted to be in his arms again, kissed into oblivion.

Caught off guard by his question, she asked him to repeat it, but couldn't form a coherent answer if her life had depended on it.

"You sound tired, and you still need to look over the changes for tomorrow. We can work on the rest of this another time."

His genial tone was deceiving. When he rose to his feet, she begged in a voice husky with longing, "Don't go."

Max said nothing, but she sensed the change in

him, a rigidity in his stance that made her wish she'd cut out her tongue.

"Dr. Rivera's hut is across the compound. It seems you're in need of his services. Judging from his behavior, he was panting for you throughout dinner. Shall I tell him to make a house call before I turn in?"

She gasped from the cruelty of his remark. "I hate you, Max Jarvis."

There was an ominous silence before he said, "You're no more capable of hating, than you are loving. There's only one thing you're good for. Pray your beauty lasts a long time, because when it fades, you'll have nothing."

The bleakness of his tone revealed a depth of pain she'd only guessed at. Long after he left the hut, Lacey lay convulsed on the cot, listening to the strange, eerie sounds of the Glades. It was a place full of living things out hunting, and being hunted.

Just then a piercing scream rent the air. It could have been her own death cry.

At the earliest possible moment, she'd go back to Salt Lake and move out of her sister's condo. Valerie would have to find someone else to house-sit. Once Lacey left Florida, she never wanted to see Max again.

CHAPTER TEN

"MOVE in closer, Lacey. That's it. There's the same monkey who's been watching you for the last week. He's above your right shoulder. Hand him the carrot. Terrific. Now pull another one from your pocket and pat your shoulder. I want to see if he'll swing from the branch and land on you."

Nick's well-modulated voice seemed to have no adverse effect on the monkey who kept scratching his head in contemplation. The other members of the crew had positioned themselves near the water to make suggestions and observe.

Suddenly Lacey got the inspiration to make a low hooting sound, mimicking George. Like magic, the monkey leaped onto her shoulder to get the other carrot.

"That's beautiful, Lacey. Whatever you're doing, keep it up."

She felt like a fool, but continued to make funny noises. The monkey stayed put long enough for Nick to get some amazing shots.

"See if he'll cling to you while you walk over to the pool."

Lacey carefully worked her way through the lush undergrowth to the edge of the blue lagoon, a place large and deep enough to accommodate a dozen people. Where the river water ran into it, a fence had been erected to keep out the alligators, making it safe for swimming.

Already Lacey had learned that the crew demanded perfection, often shooting the same scene a dozen times to get the exact shot they wanted. The work was grueling, and the sweltering heat, the insects, made conditions almost unbearable some days.

She gained a new respect for actors and models, but had no desire to become one in spite of the crew's insistence that she was a natural.

"Go over by that resurrection fern and see if the monkey will stay with you."

Lacey obeyed Nick's directive and gingerly sat down so her feet dangled in the water, afraid that any second now, the monkey would run off.

As she feared, he scrambled into some bordering mangroves. To her delight, however, he lingered nearby as if watching to see what she'd do next. On a whim, she slipped off her tennis shoes and began wading into the pool, hoping he'd follow.

All of a sudden the monkey grabbed one of her shoes and scurried to a nearby tree with his prize.

"Oh, no!" she cried, so startled by what had happened she lost her footing and fell headfirst into the water.

The guys roared with laughter, urging Nick to keep shooting. When Lacey surfaced she was laughing, as well, her sparkling eyes reflecting the primeval green of the Glades.

But Max's smile faded as she emerged from the pool, her safari outfit faithfully following every line and curve of her body. From the look in his eyes, she might as well have not been wearing anything.

Her cheeks went scarlet. She knew how his mind worked. He thought she'd planned this on purpose. No doubt he could hardly wait to castigate her.

"Let's call it a day," he said tersely.

"I'm all for that," Jeff shouted. He stripped down to his swim trunks and dove in the pool. In short order, Milo followed suit. Nick, always the joker, kicked off his shoes, and, screaming like a banshee, made a running leap into the lagoon, taking Lacey with him.

Her shrieks of laughter incited pandemonium and a huge water fight ensued. Lacey gave as good as she got, ignoring Max's thunderous glances. After a thorough dunking by Nick, she tossed her head back and discovered he'd gone.

If the others noticed, they didn't say anything. Lacey floated on her back for a while as one by one Nick and Jeff got out of the pool and started gathering their equipment. Milo was still doing laps.

"Lacey? The monkey dropped your shoe. I've put it with the other one on the side of the pool," Jeff shouted as he and Nick walked away.

"Thank goodness!" Still laughing, she tread water for a few minutes, then let out a cry which alerted Milo. He swam over to her.

"What's the matter?"

"What is it?" She pointed to something creeping through the vegetation at the other end of the pool.

"That's a panther. It's the one Ruth and Drew have

tamed. He won't hurt us. This is a water hole for all the animals and bird life in the game preserve."

True to Milo's prediction, the graceful animal made a hissing sound, then disappeared.

"I think I'm going back to the hut." She scrambled out of the water and climbed up on the grassy bank to put on her shoes.

"What's happened between you and Max?" He came straight to the point as they walked along the forest floor where the trees and vines overhead formed a cathedral-like canopy.

Her steps slowed. "I'm afraid you'd have to ask Max," she said on a choked whisper.

Milo grimaced. "We've worked together five years, but in all that time, I've never seen him in this kind of shape. For what it's worth, none of us likes the way he's been treating you, and I'm about ready to say something."

"Please don't," she pleaded. "He'll think—"

"What?" Milo demanded, sounding as imperious as Max.

Hot tears filled her eyes and splashed down her face. Her pain was so intense, she had to say something or break down completely.

"For some reason, he thinks I'm a totally promiscuous woman who could never remain faithful to one man. He despises me." Her voice shook.

Milo's eyebrows furrowed. "Is that the reason you keep your distance with me and the crew? Because Max warned you off?"

"Let's just say he manages to put a negative connotation on every move I make."

"He's a fool." Milo sounded angry.

"If you get involved, he'll only think the worst of both of us."

"Max knows I don't play around. I love my wife very much, even though we're having problems right now."

"But he's accused me of being a temptation no one can resist," she interjected bitterly.

"He's in love with you."

"Oh, no." She shook her head furiously.

"He is, but something happened in his past. Something he can't talk about, and he's letting it get in the way."

"He told me. It was a woman. She did something that made it impossible for him to love anyone. He hates me."

"You've got that wrong. He'd like to hate you."

She swallowed a sob. "It amounts to the same thing." After a pause she said, "Milo, as soon as we're through shooting, I'm going back to Salt Lake on the first available flight.

"Since you helped Jeff make all the arrangements, I wanted you to know my plans and not wonder what happened when I'm suddenly not here anymore. I trust you not to say anything to Max."

"I won't say a word." He eyed her gravely. "To quote the rest of the crew, you're one terrific lady."

Once more her face was awash with tears. "Thank you. If it weren't for the situation with Max, I'd be having the time of my life."

He put a comforting arm around her shoulder and walked her the short distance to her hut. As luck would have it, Max was outside his hut talking to Jeff as they approached. He flashed them a venomous glance.

Lacey prayed Milo would remove his arm, but to her dismay, he tightened it as if to flaunt their relationship. She understood why he did it, but he didn't have the faintest conception of what Max's anger did to her.

"Thanks for the swim," he said loud enough for Max to hear. "Let's do it again." After kissing her forehead, he strolled off. Lacey ducked inside her hut, not wanting to witness Max's reaction.

Later, while everyone ate dinner, Lacey showered and washed her hair, then hurried back to the hut in a clean pair of shorts and top, deciding to make do with fruit and crackers she kept in her room. Under no circumstances could she tolerate eating at the same table with Max.

"At last," a male voice grated as she closed the door, causing her to gasp in fright. She whirled around in anger.

"You have no right to be in here, Max."

He lounged against the dresser with his hands in his pockets, looking remote. "An unlocked door is an open invitation. I'm afraid Milo won't be making it tonight. I thought I'd offer myself instead."

The dangerous glint in his eyes caused the adrenaline to surge through her veins. At any other time in their relationship she would have been overjoyed to hear him say those words. She would have gone willingly into his arms.

But her heart had died since coming to the Glades and she wanted nothing more to do with him.

"I'm afraid I'll have to turn down your offer. Intimacy with a man who hates women as much as you do would be sacrilege."

"*Sacrilege*?" She could feel his rage boiling beneath the surface.

"Would profane be a better word?" she cried angrily. "You know nothing about me, only what your twisted mind keeps imagining. For your information, I've never been to bed with a man in my life. After getting to know you, I'm not sure the day will come that I'll ever be interested. You make me so angry. I wish to heaven I'd never met you!"

His face was a colorless mask. "You couldn't possibly wish it as much as I do. Just so you know, we're going outside the village tomorrow to shoot some scenes in the park. Your presence won't be required."

He strode from the room like an avenging prince, leaving Lacey weak and trembling.

For a minute she had to cling to the chair, too devastated by pain to move. She had no idea how long she stood there, but at some point Max's pronouncement that the crew would be away from the village the following day galvanized her into action.

She pulled things out of the dresser and started packing her bags. Every day the hospital received deliveries from Miami. She'd grab a ride into the city. From there, she would take the first flight home.

Lacey returned to the furnished attic apartment at the base of Memory Grove in downtown Salt Lake, but after living there two weeks, she still hadn't grown to like it. In fact, she had the awful premonition that no place would ever feel like home again without Max.

It had been in desperation that she had moved out of her sister's condo. She'd chosen this apartment not only because the walls and ceilings of the living room were one continuous window, giving her a breathtaking view of the city's skyline, but because of its proximity to the majority of businesses and law firms she frequented as a CPA.

Determined to cut all ties with Max, she'd bought an answering machine so that when the phone rang, she knew exactly who was calling and why. The only problem was, she hadn't yet answered the personal calls, particularly Lorraine's and Valerie's, which had been left day after day and were piling up, making her feel guilty and childish. And if she were really being honest, heartbroken.

Her new phone number was unlisted. Aside from Valerie and Lorraine, she'd only given it out to her clients, making it impossible for Max to reach her even if he'd wanted to. Which of course, he didn't!

Feeling wretched, she warmed some soup and turned on her little portable TV. Since returning from Florida, she'd refused to listen to Radio Talk. To turn on the station would be like walking through a second Gethsemane.

But it was torture *not* to listen to his show even though she knew it wasn't good for her. Tonight she'd sell her soul for the opportunity to hear his fascinating voice one more time. It was eight o'clock on a

Saturday night. All she had to do was turn on the radio and Max would invade her kitchen.

Angry with herself for even considering it, she turned off the TV, opened her briefcase and started to work. But after staring at the same ledger for ten minutes, she realized it was no use, she couldn't concentrate.

A glance at the clock told her Max's show would be over in forty-five minutes. As if her hand had a will of its own, she reached for the radio which was sitting on the counter and turned it on.

"And it never occurred to me that she wouldn't be there. Do you know how it feels to finally be ready to pour out your soul to someone, only to discover that you can't find them anywhere?"

Lacey blinked in shock because she could hear Max's voice shaking.

"So you still haven't had any luck finding Lorraine yet?"

It was a good thing Lacey was holding on to the counter with both hands.

"No. But I'm never giving up. I love her, Patsy, and I have to find her or my life's not worth living."

"That's what I said to you last month when my husband went off on another drinking binge, and you told me not to ever say that. It sounds like you need to take your own advice. Everyone has disappointments in life."

"But you don't know Lorraine, Patsy. She's the only woman in the world for me. I never considered getting married until I met her. All I want is the chance to tell her that, and to beg her forgiveness for the way I've treated her.''

Lacey thought she was going to faint.

"If she's as terrific as you say, she'll forgive you. Like you told me, nobody's perfect. Making mistakes is part of being human.''

"But I made a bad one, Patsy. So bad I can't even talk about it.''

"I understand. I'm sorry, Max. We're all rooting for you.''

"Thanks, Patsy. Call me again. Hello, you're on the air.''

"Max?''

"You're speaking to him.''

"This is Larry, the cabdriver who drove you home from the airport three weeks ago. I'm sorry to hear you're still in such bad shape. I've picked up a lot of sad fares in my time, but I have to tell Lorraine if she's out there listening, that what she did to you by moving out of her condo and leaving no forwarding address was cruel.''

"Yeah. It was cruel, but I deserved it, Larry. She was always so sweet, so loving, and all I ever did was tromp all over her feelings again and again till she couldn't take any more.''

"Well, I've got her picture, the one you gave me. I've been looking for her. If I find her, I'll call in and let you know where I saw her.''

"Thanks, Larry. I owe you big time. Now I've got to go to another call. Hello, this is the Max Jarvis show. You're on the air.''

"Hi, Max. This is Casey. Don't get too down. The

same thing happened to me, so I hired a blimp to carry a sign saying, 'Forgive me, Jean. Please marry me.' It flew over the city all day long and cost me a fortune. But it worked. She called me that night and now we're married with five kids."

"I'm happy for you, Casey. Thanks for your novel idea. My outlook has been so bleak, I just might try it. Good night, Casey. Call in anytime.

"You know, if it weren't for all you listeners out there helping me to get through this, I don't know how I'd handle it.

"The guys on my crew told me I got what I deserved and haven't been speaking to me since. When I discovered Lorraine had left Florida without telling anyone, I felt as if someone had slammed a crowbar into my gut.

"I'd finally gotten to the point where I could tell her the truth about my life, and she was gone. It's like she's disappeared off the face of the earth. Three weeks without her has been like three years. I've got to find her. I've got to make her understand. My entire life's happiness depends on it."

His pain was so tangible, Lacey felt it to her bones.

"Hello. You're on the air."

"Max?"

"*Dear God*, is it you, Lorraine?"

"No. It's Valerie."

Valerie?

Lacey was so stunned, she fell back in one of the kitchen chairs.

"When did you get back from Japan?"

"Today. I saw your message on the back door and

have been trying to call in, but the lines have been continually busy. I finally called your producer and he let me break in because I'm family."

"My producer is crazy about Lorraine, too. Have you heard from her, Valerie? Please say you have."

"No. She hasn't returned any of my calls from Tokyo, and I don't know where she's living."

Lacey heard him smother an epithet. "If she hasn't told you anything or made contact, and you're her twin sister, then I guess it's pretty hopeless."

"What you've done to her must be pretty bad. It's the first time in our lives she has refused to confide in me, and that lets me know she's in agony."

"She's not alone." The tremor in his voice reached Lacey's heart. "I have to find her and talk to her."

"My sister's the sweetest, kindest, most giving and generous human being I've ever known. One of the true innocents of the world. To see her in this kind of pain hurts me because up to now she's always been resilient and fun-loving.

"In fact she was always so happy, Daddy called her his sunshine girl. But since meeting you, she's changed. I don't know Lorraine like this and I don't think she could take being hurt any more."

"Do you think I want to hurt her?" he cried.

It was almost embarrassing to Lacey to hear Max express his innermost feelings over the airwaves. But it also touched her heart that he would humble himself and break down in front of an audience of thousands.

"If anything, my crime has been loving her too much! I refused to believe a woman like her existed until it was too late."

After a sustained pause Lacey heard her sister ask, "Have you ever told *her* that, Max?"

"I would have, but she left the Everglades while the crew and I were in the park taking pictures."

"Well, don't lose hope yet. We aren't twin sisters for nothing. She's a Radio Talk addict. I bet she's listening to you right now."

A rush of heat covered Lacey's body from head to toe.

"I pray to God you're right, Valerie."

"Listen— I have my own methods of finding her. It shouldn't take me very long."

"Just so you know, I've already contacted everyone she knows, but not even Nester or her pastor know where she's living. They'll call me as soon as they come up with anything."

He called them to help?

"I've got another idea. I'll let you in on it later. In the meantime, good luck, and if I haven't said so before, welcome to the family."

"Thanks, Valerie, even if it is premature. You don't know what that means to me. Lorraine, if you're listening... Please phone in. Without you, I'm nothing. I love you, sweetheart. Please give me one more chance."

By now the tears were falling fast and furiously.

"My producer says the calls are stacked up. Hello. You're on the air."

"Max—it's Greg."

At the sound of Greg's voice, Lacey buried her hot face in her hands.

"Does this mean you've located Lorraine?"

"Not yet, but Annette and I have been working nonstop on it. We've been keeping an eye on her usual haunts."

"I'll never be able to thank you enough, Greg."

Just how long had Max been discussing their personal lives over the air?

"Lorraine? This is Greg. Remember me? Your brother? I know you're listening. I have to tell you, you were right about us. It's Annette I love, and we're getting married at Thanksgiving, so you've got to come out of the woodwork because Annette wants you for her maid of honor.

"If you could forgive me for being such an idiot, surely you can forgive Max. The man worships the ground you walk on. What more proof do you need? Come on, Lorraine. Why don't the four of us make it a double wedding? Think about it and give in. You know you want to. You know you're dying to marry the hotshot talk host from California."

Lacey found herself laughing and crying, all at the same time.

"He's had his reasons for being so cruel. Just hear him out, Lorraine. Remember Mr. Osana in *A Majority of One*? He went over to Mrs. Jacoby's and they started all over again. Remember him saying, 'You'll accompany me to parades and concerts,' and she said, 'And you'll come to my house for Thanksgiving.' Remember how you cried, Lorraine?"

Greg. She shook her head. Trust him to quote from her favorite movie of all time. Unable to stand it another second, she phoned the business line. Rob answered.

"Rob? This is Lorraine," she said, already out of breath.

"Lorraine?" he cried in disbelief, almost damaging her eardrum. "Whatever you do, for the love of heaven, don't hang up! Max will fire me if that happens. Just hold on."

She swallowed hard, feeling frightened and excited all at the same time. "I have no intention of hanging up. Can you put me on before the end of the program? It's almost time."

"I'm transferring you now. Max is going to have a heart attack."

"Don't tell him who it is. I want to surprise him."

"Surprise is hardly the word for it. Please be nice. Life has been hell around here since he got back from his trip. He's very fragile, Lorraine," he whispered in a somber tone.

"I'll be nice. I promise."

She could hear Max saying they had time for one more call. "You're on the air. Hopefully you're one of Lorraine's clients. I've been trying to locate her through her work, but so far I've been totally unsuccessful."

Her hand shook. "H-hello, Max? I-it's Lorraine." She almost dropped the receiver. "I'm very hurt and confused, but I'm willing to talk at your place after the show."

The silence spoke volumes. When he finally made a noise, he was all choked up. "Did you listeners hear that? Lorraine's going to give me one more chance. Prayers do get answered, as her pastor said. If a miracle happens, by Tuesday afternoon I'll be able to announce that I'm getting married to the woman of my dreams.

"A wise woman named Dr. Walker called in last week to say that if I didn't start divulging something of my personal life over the air, I'd never gain credibility with my Utah audience.

"Right now I've got to work on gaining credibility in Lorraine's eyes. Wish me luck. Have a good night. I know mine's going to be one to rewrite the history books."

The next few minutes were a blur as Lacey threw on her coat, grabbed her purse and dashed out of her apartment to the car park below.

A nasty hail storm followed by pelting rain were wreaking havoc, forcing her to cross town at a snail's pace. Habits died hard as she drove around to the carport and realized Max's and Valerie's cars were in their stalls. There was no room for Lacey's.

Sighing with frustration, she rolled down her window so she could see to back out and park in front.

"Leave the car there, Lacey. Neither your sister nor I is going anywhere on a night like this."

His deep voice startled her. It seemed he knew her better than she knew herself or he wouldn't have been waiting in back. After three weeks' deprivation, the reality of his physical presence made her nervous and light-headed.

Neither of them said anything as she got out of the car. He rolled up the window and locked it, then followed her inside his condo.

Lacey walked through to the living room, experiencing an overwhelming sensation of homecoming. She didn't understand how she could feel this way when Max had done nothing but deride and humiliate her from the beginning.

"I'd help you off with your coat, but if I were to touch you right now, I wouldn't be able to stop."

With her heart practically jumping out of its cavity, Lacey lifted her head and their gazes locked. Maybe it was a trick of light, but he looked leaner in his dark trousers and sweater.

Lines at the corners of his mouth and the bruised smudges beneath his eyes gave him a gaunt appearance. She could tell he'd lost weight. Anyone who knew him would think he'd been ill, yet she found him more desirable than ever.

Unfortunately, she knew her five pound weight loss had the opposite effect, making her drawn and pale. Even her black curls lacked their usual luster.

"I came over here to ask you to stop making our private lives public. Haven't you done enough?" Her voice came out in a strangled whisper.

His jaw hardened. "I did what I had to do to find you again. All I ask is that you listen to me for five minutes. If you still want to walk out of here when I've finished, I swear I won't stop you. You'll be free of me and I'll never mention you on my show again."

Free of Max?

Unbidden tears filled her eyes and she quickly averted her head, subsiding into the nearest chair with her coat still on. "I—I know what you're going to say, Max, and I can't see that telling me about the woman who destroyed you will make the slightest bit of difference.

"You're obviously a man who can love only once. She marked you for life, and you're not capable of having a relationship with anyone else. I couldn't live with a ghost between us, because that's exactly what it would be. Deep in your heart you'll never be free of her."

To her horror, tears spilled down her cheeks like a gusher.

"In a sense, you're right," he murmured, his words like another dagger plunged into her heart. "For all her faults, my mother will always be my mother."

"Your *mother*?" Lacey's head went back and she stared at him in shock.

Slowly he nodded, but she could see he'd gone far away from her. "You're very much like her. Not in looks. But you're beautiful in the feminine way she is, you always smell divine. The way you move, the way you talk in that husky voice. Everything about you makes a man, young or old, want to carry you off to some isolated place and keep you to himself, forever."

The realization that he was talking about his mother put such a different complexion on things, Lacey was in a daze. All this time she thought he'd loved another woman and had been scarred for life.

His mouth twisted unpleasantly. "Her power was too strong for my father to resist. Unfortunately, a ring and a piece of paper meant nothing to a woman who needed, who craved, the attention and gratification of every male around.

"For so many years I believed her when she'd tell me a friend of my father's was visiting from another country. Our home was like a hotel. But until my teens, I hadn't worked it out that men only spent the night when Dad was away on business."

Lacey got to her feet, unable to contain the flood of emotions Max's words had evoked.

"One night I needed to talk over a problem with my dad, but he wasn't home. In desperation, I made the mistake of going to Mother. She was in bed with one of my dad's colleagues and didn't even know I'd opened the door. I left home that night and went to live with my best friend for a while."

"*Max—*" she whispered heartbrokenly as she watched him rake a hand through his hair.

"Dad found out where I was and came to talk to me. It was a scene I don't care to remember. When I asked him if he knew what kind of a woman Mother really was, he admitted that he did, but that she couldn't help the way she was. He needed her, and had chosen to look the other way.

"At that point in time, I think I despised my father more than my mother. In my pain, I lashed out and told him she was like a sickness with him, that no woman should ever mean more to a man than his own honor and self-respect.

"Dad tried to explain, but I couldn't handle it, and I left home for good."

"How awful for you!" she cried.

He nodded grimly. "I thought it was the end of the world. My friend's parents let me live with them until I was out of high school. I'd saved enough money from a part-time job to get me to Ceylon where I worked as a longshoreman.

"Occasionally I called Dad to keep in touch. He begged and pleaded with me to come home. He said he'd divorce Mother, but I knew he didn't mean it. Whenever she wanted to make up with him, she knew exactly how to go about it. He could never refuse an invitation to her bed."

"Didn't she ever try to get in touch with you?"

"No. I was an encumbrance. I only remember one time my father raising his voice to her. It was when he told her he thought they ought to have more children and she said one was more than enough."

"I don't believe it," Lacey murmured aghast.

He rubbed the back of his neck. "All that's in the past. I finally grew up, went to college and saw the world in the process. Through a roundabout way, it led me into broadcasting.

"I've long since reconciled my differences with Dad. Mother eventually went off with another man and I understand she's living somewhere in Australia. The good news is, when I went to see Dad last time, he informed me that he'd filed for divorce. He's met a wonderful woman and I wouldn't be surprised if he gets married again."

"Do you think he's over your mother?"

Max took a deep breath. "If he isn't, then God help him. But I don't want to talk about my parents anymore. I want to talk about us.

"You have to understand that when I first met you, I felt a quickening inside that terrified me. Without sounding conceited, I confess that in my travels and work, I've known a lot of beautiful women and have gotten close to one or two, but I'd never been hit by an instantaneous, emotional response before. It all started with your husky voice.''

"I loved your voice, too. I loved everything about you, even though your arguments infuriated me most of the time.''

"The first night you called in on the show, I knew I wanted to get to know you better. When you came to the studio as my guest, you looked at me out of those incredible green eyes, and I fell hard. But I knew I was in the most serious trouble of my life when I thought you were married to my next-door neighbor.''

A nervous hand went to her throat. "When you gave me your address, I realized you had no idea I lived next door. I couldn't wait to see you again and explain about Valerie because I was intensely attracted to you, too.''

"I know." His vibrant voice penetrated the air. "That's what was so terrible. Brad was away, and you were there, alone… I couldn't help but remember the man who slept in my father's bed while he was out of town. I was sickened by my own adulterous thoughts.''

"Now I'm beginning to understand why you were so cold to me.''

"You don't know the half of it," he groaned. "One night while I was shaving, I could hear your voice plainly through the wall. You were talking to George, talking about the trip you were going to take with him.''

It was so awful, but so funny, Lacey couldn't hold back the laughter, but it was mingled with her tears.

"You wouldn't have thought it was so hilarious if you'd been in my position," he growled, but there was a light shining in his gorgeous blue eyes. "Some man was going to sleep over and George had to hide in the storeroom, never mind that his girlfriend was missing him like crazy. And all this fooling around was going on while Brad was away."

Lacey wiped the tears from her eyes. "Oh, darling," she cried softly and reached out to him. "No wonder," she whispered, feathering his neck with avid kisses as he crushed her in his arms.

"It gets much worse," he said, his forehead against hers as he caressed her shoulders through her coat. "The minute your guest left, another man pulls up in front in a motor home, and you rush outside with a baby in your arms. You can imagine what my mind conjured up."

She could. "My guest was Brad's supervisor from Denver. I've met him dozens of times. He always sleeps at the condo when he passes through Salt Lake. As for the other man, he came from the rental car place," she confessed, brushing her lips provocatively against his. "It was for George's sake, so that we wouldn't have to be separated while I went to Idaho on business."

But she didn't get any further as Max's compelling mouth silenced hers and they clung with a long-suppressed passion. Lacey lost cognizance of her surroundings until Max stopped kissing her long enough to say, "I went a little crazy every time I saw the way men reacted around you. I was even jealous of the waiters at the hotel. As for Dr. Rivera, I could have knocked his white teeth down his throat.''

"You forgot Nester.''

"I don't want to think about him and the pictures that filled my mind of the lengths you must have gone to, to get that file from him. I don't want to remember anything. But I guess it was when I saw you in Milo's arms that something snapped and I knew I was on the verge of some kind of emotional crisis.''

She shuddered in remembered pain. "I really thought you despised me.''

He sucked in his breath and held her tighter. "That's why I left the village and spent the night in the park, to get my head on straight. I never went to sleep, and gave everything a long, hard look. By morning I knew deep in my gut that you were totally innocent.

"It hit me then that you loved me and that I was terrified I'd destroyed the woman I loved more than life itself. I couldn't get back to the village fast enough. But my worst nightmare became reality because you'd gone.''

She wrapped her arms around his neck. "I had to leave. You made it clear you hated me, but I kept letting you do your worst because I couldn't bear to give you up.''

He shook his dark blond head. "Lacey, you've got to forgive me,'' he begged in a hoarse whisper.

"Now that I know what was driving you, there's nothing to forgive. I love you too much, and I want to make up for all your pain.''

"I don't deserve you."

"Hush." She quieted his lips with her own, rejoicing in the right to touch this man, to love him for the rest of her life.

Again they were caught away in a tide so powerful, it threatened to consume her. His caressing hand found the buttons of her coat. Like magic it slipped from her shoulders and fell to the floor in a heap.

"Dear Lord, how I've needed this. I love you, Lacey. So much I could never, *ever*, share you with anyone else. I'm not like my father."

Marveling at his vulnerability, her hands shaped the contours of his firm jaw and held him fast while the light of love burned in her brilliant green eyes.

"There's no one else. Greg was like a brother, and not even Perry could coax me into bed. I'm a one-man woman, and I love only you, want only you. No matter how awful you were to me, I've never been happier in my life than when we were living together.

"That's why I'm here. I adore you, Max. Do you believe me?" Her voice throbbed with the urgency of her question. Her entire future rested on his answer.

At last, incredibly, tears filled his eyes. He stared at her for a long, long time. "Yes. I believe you. I think I've believed it since the moment you introduced me to George, but I was so embittered by Mother's behavior, I refused to admit you were her antithesis."

His words released her pent-up emotions. Lacey had nothing but love to give him as her body molded to his. They swayed together from the sheer ecstasy of their embrace.

"I've been in agony over the love I feel for you. Make the pain go away, Max."

"It'll go away, I'll see to it personally," he vowed in fierce tones, drowning her in kisses until she couldn't breathe. "But not until our honeymoon, and that means a church wedding with you dressed in white, surrounded by family and friends. After all my suspicions, I need to atone for my sins. Besides, I wouldn't want to scandalize Mrs. Taggert. She's one of my fans and has been searching for you, as well."

"Making our private life public probably drew in another hundred thousand listeners," she teased, pressing hungry kisses to his enticing mouth.

"Naturally. I'm going to marry Lorraine, Radio Talk's sweetheart. That makes me an insider now."

She flashed him a saucy smile. "Did you talk your boss into letting you do this? Is that why you're really marrying me?"

But her teasing smile slowly faded as she saw the raw blaze of desire flare in his eyes, igniting her own passionate nature.

"I'll answer your question when I take you to bed for the first time, Mrs. Jarvis. That kind of heart talk is reserved for husbands and wives *only*."

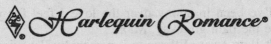

Harlequin Romance ®

is pleased to offer

SIMPLY THE BEST

Authors you'll treasure, books you'll want to keep!

These are romances we know you'll love reading—
over and over again! Because they are,
quite simply, the best....

Watch for these special books by some of your
favorite authors:

#3468 WILD AT HEART
by Susan Fox (August 1997)

#3471 DO YOU TAKE THIS COWBOY?
by Jeanne Allan (September 1997)

#3477 NO WIFE REQUIRED!
by Rebecca Winters (October 1997)

Available in August, September and October 1997
wherever Harlequin books are sold.

Every month there's another title from one
of your favorite authors!

October 1997
Romeo in the Rain by Kasey Michaels
When Courtney Blackmun's daughter brought home Mr. Tall,
Dark and Handsome, Courtney wanted to send the young
matchmaker to her room! Of course, that meant the single
New Jersey mom would be left alone with the irresistibly
attractive Adam Richardson....

November 1997
Intrusive Man by Lass Small
Indiana's Hannah Calhoun had enough on her hands taking
care of her young son, and the last thing she needed was a
man complicating things—especially Max Simmons, the
gorgeous cop who had eased himself right into her little boy's
heart...and was making his way into hers.

December 1997
Crazy Like a Fox by Anne Stuart
Moving in with her deceased husband's—*eccentric*—family
in Louisiana meant a whole new life for Margaret Jaffrey and
her nine-year-old daughter. But the beautiful young widow
soon finds herself seduced by the slower pace and the much-
too-attractive cousin-in-law, Peter Andrew Jaffrey....

**BORN IN THE USA: Love, marriage—
and the pursuit of family!**

Available at your favorite retail outlet!

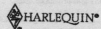 

Don't miss these Harlequin favorites
by some of our bestselling authors! Act now and
receive a discount by ordering two or more titles!

HT#25720	A NIGHT TO REMEMBER	$3.50 U.S.	☐
	by Gina Wilkins	$3.99 CAN.	
HT#25722	CHANGE OF HEART	$3.50 U.S.	☐
	by Janice Kaiser	$3.99 CAN.	
HP#11797	A WOMAN OF PASSION	$3.50 U.S.	☐
	by Anne Mather	$3.99 CAN.	
HP#11863	ONE-MAN WOMAN	$3.50 U.S.	☐
	by Carole Mortimer	$3.99 CAN.	
HR#03356	BACHELOR'S FAMILY	$2.99 U.S.	☐
	by Jessica Steele	$3.50 CAN.	
HR#03441	RUNAWAY HONEYMOON	$3.25 U.S.	☐
	by Ruth Jean Dale	$3.75 CAN.	
HS#70715	BAREFOOT IN THE GRASS	$3.99 U.S.	☐
	by Judith Arnold	$4.50 CAN.	
HS#70729	ANOTHER MAN'S CHILD	$3.99 U.S.	☐
	by Tara Taylor Quinn	$4.50 CAN.	
HI#22361	LUCKY DEVIL	$3.75 U.S.	☐
	by Patricia Rosemoor	$4.25 CAN.	
HI#22379	PASSION IN THE FIRST DEGREE	$3.75 U.S.	☐
	by Carla Cassidy	$4.25 CAN.	
HAR#16638	LIKE FATHER, LIKE SON	$3.75 U.S.	☐
	by Mollie Molay	$4.25 CAN.	
HAR#16663	ADAM'S KISS	$3.75 U.S.	☐
	by Mindy Neff	$4.25 CAN.	
HH#28937	GABRIEL'S LADY	$4.99 U.S.	☐
	by Ana Seymour	$5.99 CAN.	
HH#28941	GIFT OF THE HEART	$4.99 U.S.	☐
	by Miranda Jarrett	$5.99 CAN.	

(limited quantities available on certain titles)

	TOTAL AMOUNT	$ _____
DEDUCT:	**10% DISCOUNT FOR 2+ BOOKS**	$ _____
	POSTAGE & HANDLING	$ _____
	($1.00 for one book, 50¢ for each additional)	
	APPLICABLE TAXES*	$ _____
	TOTAL PAYABLE	$ _____

(check or money order—please do not send cash)

To order, complete this form and send it, along with a check or money order for the total above, payable to Harlequin Books, to: **In the U.S.:** 3010 Walden Avenue, P.O. Box 9047, Buffalo, NY 14269-9047; **In Canada:** P.O. Box 613, Fort Erie, Ontario, L2A 5X3.

Name: _____

Address: _____ City: _____

State/Prov.: _____ Zip/Postal Code: _____

*New York residents remit applicable sales taxes.
Canadian residents remit applicable GST and provincial taxes.

Look us up on-line at: http://www.romance.net

HARLEQUIN WOMEN KNOW ROMANCE WHEN THEY SEE IT.

And they'll see it on **ROMANCE CLASSICS**, the new 24-hour TV channel devoted to romantic movies and original programs like the special **Harlequin® Showcase of Authors & Stories.**

The **Harlequin® Showcase of Authors & Stories** introduces you to many of your favorite romance authors in a program developed exclusively for Harlequin® readers.

Watch for the **Harlequin® Showcase of Authors & Stories** series beginning in the summer of 1997.

If you're not receiving ROMANCE CLASSICS, call your local cable operator or satellite provider and ask for it today!

ROMANCE CLASSICS

Escape to the network of your dreams.

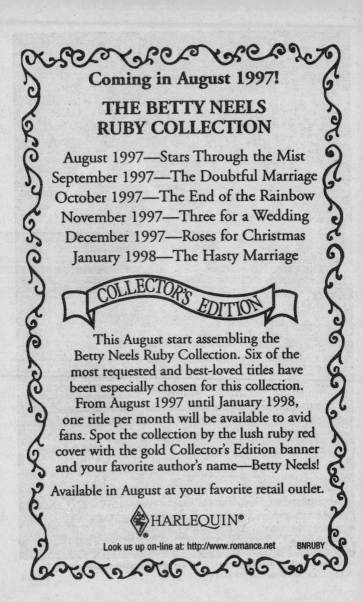